Shine

LEANNE ACIZ STANTON

Printed in the United States of America
Published by L A S Press
Cover photo taken by Renee Jackson
Cover embellishment made by Kaitlynn DeWitt
ISBN: 978-0-9967256-7-5
Library of Congress Control Number: 2015914186

10 9 8 7 6 5 4 3 2 1

Author's Note

Some situations in this novel were inspired by real events, but all of the characters are works of fiction. Names, dates, some locations, personality traits, characteristics, and details have all been invented for creative purposes. Real places, real music, real TV shows, real movies and real products appear throughout, but the characters, what they do and what they say, are the products of the author's imagination. Any resemblance to actual persons, living or dead, is purely coincidental.

Dedicated to Mark

A-Side

B-Side

VIII

Per Aspera Ad Astra;
"Through Hardships To The Stars"

The Mall And Misery

I remember where we were. I was with my mother, my Aunt Caroline, and my cousin Nicholas who was younger than me. We were driving to the mall for an afternoon of shopping. The trees zoomed by as my aunt remarked about all of the garage sales that we passed and how she always found her "best deals" at them. We laughed as my cousin and I played with his Teenage Mutant Ninja Turtle figurines in the backseat. My cousin had shiny black hair and it swayed from side to side every time he giggled.

Nicholas began to tell a story about something his father had done earlier in the day, something that had particularly amazed his young mind. He thought to himself for a moment, and then turned to look at me and asked, "Where's your daddy, Ellie?"

With those words, all of the air in the car sucked out

and I was blinded by what I can only define now as my harsh reality.

We had been staying at my aunts for my birthday weekend in northern New Jersey. My Aunt Caroline had slaved over making two different cakes for the occasion, one with chocolate frosting and the other, a vanilla-coconut custard cake. I was handed what seemed like a gazillion gifts to open and then we moved to the kitchen.

I galloped in, sat down, stretched my arms out over the brown oak table and enjoyed the moment as my family delightfully sang the happy birthday song to me. I looked at my aunt next to her husband and thought to myself how odd it was that my mother was alone, while my aunt and uncle were together...but I wanted to eat cake, so I brushed it off.

I had noticed the day before and so had Nicholas. This young boy realized that while he was used to parents coming in pairs, mine did not. He was confused and so was I.

I was speechless, and tried to stammer out a response when my Aunt Caroline quietly explained, "Ellie's daddy passed away." I saw my mother tighten her lips in the rearview mirror, but she kept quiet.

Nicholas looked at me wide-eyed and began to shoot questions off to his mother. What did "pass way" mean? Where did he go? Was he coming back? I already knew what it meant to pass away...it meant you were dead.

While my aunt nervously hushed my cousin's questions, I lost myself looking out the window, coming to terms with a fact that I had never realized before. It had always been just my mom and I, and I liked it that way. We were best friends, we had so much fun together, but...where did my daddy go? How did he die? Most importantly, if I prayed enough or wished hard enough, could I bring him back?

I thought of all the birthday parties and school events that just my mother had been there for, in a sea of proud parents that included both mothers and fathers. All of the parent teacher meetings my mother went to alone. All of those snowy nights where my mother had to shovel out her own car, while the other women on my block had their husbands do it for them.

It was heartbreaking.

We finally arrived at the mall. After searching through about four lanes, we found a spot and proceeded to climb out of the car. My mother grabbed me and hugged me with tears in her eyes. I found comfort in my mother's arms, but nothing could ever change the fact that that day, I realized that my daddy wasn't around and

he was never coming back.

*

Oh right, my father's death. That's a pretty important piece of my story so I might as well just leap right into it.

My mother and father went to the same high school in the 70's. Both hippies, they met each other at a school board meeting that was being held to determine whether or not high school girls should be allowed to play on the high school boys athletic teams. My mother, the rebellious kind of hippie (peace, love, and a little war) had started an accidental uproar in her high school after trying out for the boy's football team and being told she couldn't, so she organized a board meeting with the faculty and the mayor to discuss the situation.

My father had heard about a girl from his school causing commotion over the athletic teams and though my father was no athlete, he went with some friends to watch this chick fight for her cause. When my mother confidently walked in prepared with a folder full of rules and regulations of high school sports, my father was immediately intrigued - not by her beauty, but by her intelligence.

Like a heartsick teenage boy, my father began to show up at all of the hangouts my mother went to. There were hundreds of girls in their high school that had crushes on my handsome father – but all he wanted was my mother, an Ali McGraw lookalike, who was as fiery as she was beautiful. He asked her out and after a few times of being told she wasn't allowed to date, my mother decided to ignore her parents wishes and date him anyway.

My father wrote my mother poetry with Sharpie markers on paper that was ripped out of magazines and cooked her meals that were impressive coming from a high school student. Apparently, my father was a great cook. From what I hear from every person who has ever known my father, he was also the nicest guy in the world, which explains why the local florists in town ran out of flowers after his wake.

That's not to say that my parents were the All-American

high school sweethearts that people normally think of. With my mother being a rebel who was wise beyond her years due to her upbringing, she certainly gave him a run for his money. My mother stayed away from drugs and drinking, scared to catch a beating if she ever came home anything but sober, and she would grow frustrated at my father's weekend partying. Still, they loved each other with the kind of young love that my mother remarked 'most people only dream about' and she ran with it, throwing caution to the wind.

My mother's father, my grandfather, didn't approve of my father because he knew of his reputation, so eventually my mother moved out after she graduated high school, leaving her siblings behind to live with my father. It was a tough decision leaving her family, but my mother was headstrong and determined to begin her adult life. My father proposed in their early twenties and my parents got married, much to the exasperation of my grandfather.

My mother had a tough time adjusting to being someone's wife but she adapted, while still being what she really was, which was strong-willed. A good example of a rebel trying to become domesticated is when my mother went to the local supermarket to get food to make my father a grand rib eye steak dinner after they had just gotten married. She was excited to surprise her husband with an impressive, delicious dinner (considering it was usually my father who did the cooking) and after scouring through recipe books, she ran to the supermarket to pick up the necessary ingredients.

Once she got home and started to prepare, she realized the steak was rotting, so she went back to the store to see if she could exchange it for fresh meat. It should have been a simple exchange but instead, the only working manager told her, "I'm sorry, I don't have a second to spare. I'm busy." My disappointed mother left with rotting meat, only to catch that manager sneaking a cigarette outside as she walked towards her car. As soon as she got home, she angrily called in a false bomb threat to the store: now that guy really wouldn't have a second to spare.

Eventually my parents settled down in an apartment on Paper Street in Meadows, a small suburban town in New Jersey, a few miles away from where they had both grown up. My mother worked various jobs, while my father built houses around New Jersey, one beer at a time.

During the holidays before I was born, my father would cook delicious meals big enough to feed an army, and he would host all of their friends in their tiny apartment. My father was so gratuitous, he even invited the town drunks so they had a place to eat and let them crash so they wouldn't wake up on Thanksgiving Day in a Salvation Army box or on the street. Sure, there were questionable characters, but my mother recounts these nights as "good times".

I was born on the same day as my mother, who called me her "favorite birthday gift". My parents named me Elodie (pronounced like melody) but my father called me Ellie for short and the nickname stuck. My mother instantly matured once I came along and she began to revolve her life around me, spending her hard earned money on baby stuff instead of on fedoras and luxurious suits for my father. Alcohol and drugs ran rampant at this time and my father was becoming a functional alcoholic. My father was still in his twenties and didn't want the party to end, so even though he adored me more than anything, he continued to hang out with his friends, drinking and staying out all night.

My father eventually became a bar fly, you know the ones. The ones who stop at the bar for a beer before going home, only to end up spending the entire night there, eventually heading home to an irate spouse. The kind who didn't care much about how irate their spouse was, simply because giving in to alcoholism made it impossible to care about anyone else but yourself.

One night, he stopped in a local bar on the other side of town to make a phone call. Benny Black, a man who was known around town for being a bizarre, unpredictable drug addict, was there and he had a score to settle with my father in regards to an argument they had a few weeks earlier. During his high school years, Black would exhibit many symptoms of a person with mental illness, like abusing animals and having manic fits during class. Once he developed into an addict, he became a different kind of crazy.

My father made his phone call and got up to leave. As he waved goodbye to all of his friends who smiled back at him with a nod, he didn't notice Black get up behind him. He continued to walk outside and took a deep breath, enjoying the spring air. He heard a noise behind him and turned around.

It was Black, smashing his fist into the back of my father's head, much to his surprise. My father fell, and Black proceeded to kick my father in the head with his construction work boots. After fourteen kicks, it was only then that Black stopped.

*

My father lay in the hospital for a few days, fighting his coma. My family was beside themselves with grief. My mother had been back and forth to the hospital, pleading with my father to wake up, to no avail. She felt hopeless. My mother felt bad that she was spending so much time at the hospital and not with me, so she decided to take Nicholas and I for ice cream one day after school. She held our hands, securing our way crossing the street, and we all jumped in our seats, buckling in our seat belts.

It was then that she saw him: Benny Black, walking down the street, without a care in the world. The guy that had just put her husband, her daughter's father, in a coma that doctors didn't think he would ever come out of. The guy that had turned her world upside down by destroying any possibility of her family living happily ever after. The guy who was going back to the scene of the crime because he was that much of a drunk.

He noticed us and hanging his head low, began to sprint. My mother drove her car next to him, edging closely into his denim jeans, screaming, "You coward, attacking my husband when his back was turned!"

People stopped and stared. They didn't know who to feel bad for – the near-widow of the nicest guy in the town, or the guy who had put her husband in a coma that she was berating. So, they said nothing.

"I HOPE YOU PAY FOR THIS!" My mother continued screaming, following him the entire time, still edging her car into him from the sidewalk. He arrived at his destination, the same bar he had nearly killed my father at, and ran inside. He was safe. He knew my mother wouldn't follow him into THAT bar with her daughter and nephew in the car, alone. Shaking, my mother proceeded to get us ice cream and we ate in painful silence.

Hours later, my mother received a phone call from a Meadows cop. They were calling to let her know Black had gone to the police station to press charges on her for harassment and she was going to have to give a statement at some point. In a huff, my mother grabbed her purse and went down to the station.

"Ma'am, you can't be doing this kind of stuff. We know you're upset but this is not the way to handle it," one of the cops pleaded with my mother when she arrived at the station, ready to start a war. Benny Black was already awaiting charges on attempted manslaughter, so it was best for my mother to let him dig his own grave and not add fuel to the fire.

At 2:17 in the morning, my father died. I was three years old.

I didn't go to the services, but everybody else in Meadows did. The line wrapped around the funeral home.

Cold Desert

While awaiting a highly anticipated trial for my father's case, Benny Black stabbed his wife to death during an argument while his children were peacefully asleep in their bedrooms downstairs. Alerted to the screams of their mother, the children ran to their parent's bedroom to find their mother's bloody corpse and their father missing.

"Local Woman Stabbed To Death By Husband"
Excerpt from the news: Benny Black, the victim's husband, has been charged in the death of his wife for the brutal slaying that occurred last week. His young children found their mother unresponsive and bloody, and ran to their neighbor's house screaming to call 911. Black was later found unconscious in the bushes a few blocks away.

Suddenly, our close-knit neighborhood was thrust into the spotlight for being the hometown of a murderer with psychopathic tendencies. His parents were ashamed and humiliated for not getting him the psychiatric help he had needed since he was a child and Meadows residents quickly turned their backs to them. My mother, devastated and now a widow, was determined to see Black end up in prison where he belonged so he couldn't ruin any more lives.

Thus began two of the longest and most-grueling legal battles ever in New Jersey: the state of New Jersey versus Benny Black. The trial for my father's death would go on for several years. My dark drawings would be submitted as evidence as to how the loss of my father and the understanding of death affected me. My father's friends would be subpoenaed to testify as witnesses. Defense attorneys for Black would argue that my father's wild lifestyle of drinking heavily and partying were the main reason for his death and not the malicious beating caused by Black himself.

Of course, a person with common sense would argue that the coma and his eventual demise were brought on because of the attack by Black. It was basic read-between-the-lines: my father was living his day to day life just fine before the fight, regardless of his drinking habits. Suffering from over fourteen powerful blows to the head by a kicking work boot was the real reason, not the fact that because of his lifestyle, it was hard for his body to replenish itself after being attacked.

'If he hadn't been attacked, he'd still be here today' was a statement argued consistently over the next few years. The trial became so heated that at one point our lawyer pointed in Black's face and screamed, "MURDERER, MURDERER, MURDERER!" I would find out many years later that several law programs use this trial as an example in their courses.

Bold and blaring front page headlines during the trial read:

"Trial opens in bar fight case"
Excerpt: "Talk about tragedy," the prosecutor said during opening statements. "This man's need to make a phone call cost him his life."

"Black's lawyer fails to kill charges"
Excerpt: Black is facing life in state prison if convicted of murder. He faces another murder trial later this year, for the death of his wife. The state contends – in what will be a capital murder trial – that Black argued with his wife, who had requested a divorce and secured a restraining order against him, only to stab her to death while their children slept nearby.

"Kicks in the head killed man, state doctor testifies"
Excerpt: State Coroner testified that the victim was kicked so hard his brain was dented and bruised. "Nobody gets spontaneous multiple trauma like the ones in this specific case unless it is caused by pointed, excessive force," the state medical examiner that did the victim's autopsy testified in court. "The victim's injuries are consistent with someone who received direct blows to the head."

"Man accused of murder testifies in own defense"
Excerpt: The state intends to prove that Black, who was

wearing steel toe work boots, punched the victim once from behind, knocking him down, then repeatedly kicked him in the head while he was stretched out on the ground, helpless. The victim rolled towards the door, where Black pulled him back and kicked him again.

"Jury to decide if Black is a murderer"

Excerpt: Jurors will not know Black's prior indictment for the murder of his wife whom he allegedly stabbed to death.

"Black found guilty:
Beats murder rap, nailed on assault"

Excerpt: The defense attorney said that Black's acquittal on murder charges for the victim would help in the trial he faces later this year for allegedly killing his wife. "The fact that he was acquitted of this first murder charge lets him into the next case without the burden of a prior murder conviction."

The state of New Jersey was outraged. Many people knew my father as a kind man and regardless of his alcoholism, he was a good person. Many people also knew that Benny Black was not...and at the very least, he was mentally ill. How could the state of New Jersey let him go convicted of only assault, considering that he eventually stabbed his wife to death? The jurors that were deciding this man's fate were not privy to the other murder, so it was blamed on a technicality. It was injustice in the legal system at its very finest.

At the end of all of these newspaper clippings, there was

a letter to the editor submitted by my mother, days after the verdict was released.

<u>BLACK VERDICT ATROCIOUS</u>

This letter is in response to the 'slap on the wrist' the Benny Black jurors decided to give to him. This unbelievable verdict was also a 'slap in the face' to the victim's family.

I write this letter in disbelief at the legal system. We waited a long time for this trial, only to see quite clearly my husband's lifestyle was on trial and not Black's violent past.

You see, Black's rights were protected and none of this could be brought up in front of jurors. To have him portrayed as an innocent patron at a bar is almost laughable. His attorney was happy with this verdict, knowing this charge could be admissible in Black's pending trial for "allegedly" stabbing his wife to death.

His attorney called the jurors "conscientious and attentive." I call them "listless and bored". Perhaps they missed the respected coroner say that the beating bruised and dented the victim's brain.

As the victim's widow and mother of his little girl, I am heartsick and appalled by the verdict. How did this "conscientious and attentive" jury feel the next day when they read the paper and read about the trial he has pending? Was at least one remorseful and ashamed of the 'slap on the wrist' verdict?

God,

I hope so.

Sincerely,

"The Victim's" Wife

*

Benny Black was eventually fully charged in the death of his wife and found guilty of assault against my father. He avoided the death penalty that prosecutors originally sought, but he rots in jail to this day. As an adult, I would be told by a man who had been in prison with Black that my father's killer endured harsh daily beatings from other inmates for various reasons. Regardless of how my father's death would impact my life throughout the years, knowing this, I felt a sort of sympathy for Black - but I felt worse for his children who had to live the rest of their lives just like my mother and I did...connected to this tragedy forever.

*

In kindergarten, I got into an argument with a boy I went to school with while playing kickball. I was the captain of my team and we were winning. The other team's captain appeared jealous and after some senseless juvenile smack-talk, he told me sharply, "At least my father isn't dead." The wind sucked out of my sails at the realization that not only did I know my father was gone, but so did everyone else. Wasn't it bad enough that I didn't have a dad and most of my peers did? Now I had to be teased over it? I ran into the bathroom and cried.

Another time, one of the girls in my class informed me of how my father died and who had killed him while we were sitting on the grass, playing with Polly Pockets. I was dazed out in playing when I caught the last few words of her conversation.

"...We should make the bad guy's name be Benny Black," she finished.

"Who is Benny Black?" I asked, pushing my Polly figurine into her bathroom to take a shower. I had heard that name somewhere before.

"The man who killed your dad. My parents say he was a real bad guy," she replied. I shuddered at the words "bad guy".

My head shot up. Up until that moment, I had never asked how my father died, nor had anybody told me. Somebody had killed him?

"How did he kill him?" I inquired, looking back at my Polly Pocket, embarrassed to have to ask this girl for information on my own father.

"He beat up your dad," she answered. She put her figurine to bed and looked at me.

"How do you know?" I asked defensively.

"My mom and dad were talking about it. My mom said your dad got kicked in the head and then died, " she said.

"That's not true," I replied, not knowing if it was or wasn't.

"Yes it is," she insisted.

"No it's not," I said, getting angry.

"Ask your mom then," she said, shrugging.

I crossed my arms and stalked off, counting down the minutes until the end of the school day when my mother would pick me up so I could ask her myself. Once the bell rang, I raced towards my mother when she came to the door to retrieve me from my teacher. I stared at her, and sensing that I had something to say, she asked me what was wrong. I continued to stare as she bent down, looking me directly in the eyes. I said nothing but deep down, I was angry that everybody knew how my father died and I didn't, even though I didn't really want to know. She sighed as she took my hand and changed the subject.

This began an uncomfortable child-like fascination with my father's death and my understanding of it. When walking around my hometown with my mother, I would stare at strangers and wonder if they were the man who had killed my father. When my teacher would tell the class to use a black crayon, I would refuse and use every other color. My teacher was concerned about my resistance to the color black, but knowing my back story made her give me space and she told my mother it was just a phase.

Sensing my uneasiness was more than just a phase, my mother sat me down one day at the kitchen table and said, "Ellie, I think it's time we talk about what happened to your father."

I threw my hands up to my ears and covered them, singing loudly, "LaLaLaLaLaLa." She tried to pull my hands away but I kept them stuck to my ears, pretending they were glued there. My mother tried a few more times to bring it up, only to get the same reaction out of me: me covering my ears and running away. I knew that the conversation would be uncomfortable and awkward, and besides, I didn't need to know anyway. Knowing the truth wouldn't change things, it would just hurt me more.

I wouldn't understand the real impact of my father's absence until I was older. Many times, I would run into old friends of my father's who wouldn't even be able to say the word "hello" without tearing up. I didn't understand why these grown adults would get emotional at the sight of me, mainly because I didn't understand that while I had lost a father who I had few memories with, these people had lost a friend who they had tons of memories with. It was depressing running into these people as a child and whenever we did, I would tug on my mother's purse in urgency, much to her relief.

I didn't find out the whole story behind my father's death until many years later when I eventually came across a red leather envelope that fell to my feet when I went into my mother's closet to look for something. I opened it gingerly, surprised as tons of newspaper clippings, hospital records, and cemetery deeds fell out. Realizing what they were, I paused for a moment, knowing that once I went through these papers, I could never go back to innocence and oblivion.

It was time. I sat with my legs crossed on my mother's bedroom floor and read through each document, my eyes filling with the truth as I finally put together the missing pieces of the puzzle.

Black Velvet

My mother was, and still is, literally the toughest person I know: mentally, emotionally, and physically. In fact, I've never met a man with more balls than my mother. Throughout many events in my life I would witness people cower down to her, as if they didn't want to engage in a confrontation they wouldn't win. They knew better.

My mother had it rough growing up poor in Palisades, an urban town in New Jersey. My mother and her siblings were left to fend for themselves for most of their childhood – until my grandfather was made aware of the circumstances his children were living under with his ex-wife and saved them. My Aunt Maureen (my mother's oldest sister) recounts stories of the winters when she was young and had to walk in the snow to beg for food so her younger siblings would be able to eat.

My mother and her siblings endured various forms of

traumatizing neglect, which would forever impact the rest of their lives and trickle down. The stories my cousins and I were told when we were growing up sounded more like nightmares than real-life. These were the kinds of stories that your parents tell you to make you realize how much luckier you are then when they were your age and how easy you really have it… except these stories were actually true.

Out of her siblings, my mother took on the protector role. Thanks to this, her siblings were protected from whoever and whatever they needed protection from. It wasn't unheard of to hear my mother had gone after girls from the hood – and won.

One day during high school, my aunt was late from school. My mother and her siblings had a strict curfew and they knew better than to dismiss it. My grandfather and my mother waited outside the house for my aunt, only to see her limping and bloodied, walking up the street. It was clear she had been in a fight.

"I got jumped by a bunch of girls down by the park! They beat me up and I told them, wait till my sister finds out about this, she's going to get you!" my aunt sobbed, showing off the footprint on her stomach.

The next day, my mother went into school enraged. She walked from locker to locker, looking for the girls who had jumped my aunt, who also happened to be in her grade. After being given a tip that the girls were probably in the bathroom smoking cigarettes, my mother sprinted there and sure enough, they were.

My mother opened the door, closed it behind her, and

crossed her arms. There were five girls staring back at my mother, silently daring her to do something. They suspected my mother would come looking for them and they thought they had strength in numbers. My mother, without saying a word, started barreling on these chicks. In her words, she "went ballistic." She was so fast, they couldn't keep up. Even with the fact that my mother was clearly outnumbered, she beat the shit out of these girls, ending it with barely a scratch on her body.

A male teacher, alerted to the fight, rushed in and smacked my mother across the face to stop the commotion. My aunts were also made aware of the fight and were stunned to get there and see this grown man slap their sister across the face in front of everybody. My mother didn't even bat an eyelash, she was just happy she had taught those girls a resounding lesson: don't mess with her family.

"That's the last time those girls mess with you," my mother said to my aunt unfazed, gathering her dark hair back into a neat ponytail.

Oh, and it was. Grandpa didn't raise no fool.

*

My grandfather was an extraordinary guy. A tough Korean War veteran, he smoked Marlboro Reds and rocked some questionable tattoos, like Looney Tune characters on his forearm. He ate Twizzlers, loved his dogs more than most humans, and there was always a dusty drill on the table, waiting to be used at a moment's notice. His voice was loud but he spoke with love, most of the time without a shirt on, his belly protruding over his denim jeans. He talked to my mother and her siblings like they were still teenagers, even though they were now married with kids. I had a great example of a loving father from my grandfather.

I spent a lot of time with my grandfather and his wife, who I considered my grandma, since my mother had long-ago cut ties with her own mother. They lived in Boiling Springs in an old blue Victorian house, which was the same house my mother and her siblings spent their teenage years after my grandfather rescued them from their mother.

My grandfather's house was huge. The backyard was a kid's dream, full of toys in a huge yard with a ground pool. Most of my summers growing up would be spent swimming, dodging my cousins jumping off of the nearby roof into the pool and playing endless games of Marco Polo. My mother and aunts would sit nearby, tanning and watching us while my uncles would smoke cigars in the yard and talk about cars and football. Next to the pool was a garage that was turned into a huge doghouse for my grandfather's dogs. My grandfather's vicious dogs were notorious, simply because he always had so many different kinds.

One Easter, my mother ran out to grab milk for my grandma, who was preparing a feast and needed it for mashed potatoes. My grandfather was busy watching some game and I was the first grandkid to arrive, so I had nobody to play with yet. With my developing Attention Deficit Disorder, that got boring quickly. I decided I was going to go outside while I waited for everyone else to arrive. I opened the creaky white screen door and waved off my grandma, who was yelling something I couldn't make out.

I wandered around the yard a bit, kicked some balls, and looked for ladybugs on the shrubs. Boring. One of the dogs barked and I turned my head over, suddenly fascinated by the three dogs panting away. I walked over, peering at them over the fence. There was a Rottweiler, a German Shepherd, and a Doberman. They seemed nice enough. I had never gotten close enough to the dogs (us kids weren't allowed near the garage) to know that these dogs were not friendly because they were guard dogs, trained to eat intruder's faces off and leave them for dead.

I decided, because apparently my brain disappeared for a few minutes, to walk into the dog's den, regardless of the bold red sign that read "Do Not Open". I unlocked the (in my opinion, not-so-childproof) lock and walked in, hoping to make some furry friends.

...I didn't.

One of the dogs attacked me and went for my head.

Chaos ensued.

I screamed.

The dogs barked like maniacs.

My grandma ran out, screaming.

My grandfather limped out, screaming.

Blood. Lots and lots of blood.

Back then, my mother had some great fashion sense and she dressed me accordingly. In one of my Child Development Team reports, it's noted that "Elodie is always impeccably dressed. She wears a constant array of velvet dresses, complete with stockings and Mary Jane shoes. She is always dressed to the nines and I think her mother takes pride in that."

If my mother dressed me in velvet dresses and Mary Jane's for school, you could imagine the kind of outfit she had me decked out in for Easter. It was like every day was a beauty pageant, except my baby fat would disqualify me in the first round. So when my mother came strolling up the driveway carrying a gallon of milk and saw all of the blood gushing from my head onto my dress, she dropped it on the ground to burst everywhere, running towards me like a bat out of hell.

Again, more chaos ensued.

Screaming. LOTS of screaming. No hospital visit, but tons of screaming.

My mother to my grandfather: "WHY THE !@#$ WAS SHE OUTSIDE WITHOUT ANYONE WATCHING HER?"

My grandfather to my grandma: "WHY THE !@#$

WEREN'T YOU WATCHING HER OUTSIDE?"

My grandma to me: "WHY THE !@#$ DIDN'T YOU LISTEN TO ME WHEN I WAS TELLING YOU NOT TO GO BY THE DOGS WHEN YOU WENT OUTSIDE?"

Oh, so that's what she had said! Easter was ruined...and now, we needed milk. Again.

*

Another Easter, my Uncle Lenny (a teenager at the time) took my younger cousins and I for a walk around the block so he could sneakily smoke a cigarette. It was the first time I could be trusted out of my mom's eyesight and I was excited to go on this adventure. We jumped on the uneven concrete, swiped at the bees, and admired the humongous houses that Boiling Springs had to offer. We held hands tightly, laughing the whole time and eventually returned back to my grandfather's house, where my mother was getting out of her car. She looked sad.

"Mommy! We walked around the block by ourselves!" I beamed with pride.

"That's good!" she said, robotically.

"Where were you?" I asked.

"Visiting your father," she answered, tired of the thought.

"Oh," I replied blankly, not knowing what that meant. How was she visiting him? I thought he was dead. Where was he?

"At the cemetery, where he is buried," my mother answered, sensing my confusion.

"What does buried mean?" I asked. My Uncle Lenny shifted uncomfortably, pushing my younger cousins to follow him in the house, leaving my mother and I to ourselves.

"When people pass away, we say our goodbyes and then we put them in the ground to rest in peace," my mother said carefully.

"Oh," I answered. How was being in the ground for the rest of eternity resting in peace?

"You've been to the cemetery before, you just don't remember it."

Silence.

"Do you want to go later?" my mother asked.

"No."

"Let's go."

"Okay..."

We went and ate Easter dinner with my family, both of us with knots in our stomachs. I wanted to pause time and prolong the meal because I was scared to go to the cemetery, but I knew that I had to. It was then that I realized that every holiday we had spent at my grandfather's, my mother had snuck out to visit my father who was buried in the cemetery nearby. Alone.

When dinner was over, I reluctantly hopped in the car and stared out the window for the drive. My mother looked at me through the rearview mirror for what must have been at least ten times. We went to the cemetery, a scene I compared to an overflowing sea of lonely headstones. I saw his grave and we stood there in silence both staring ahead. It was the first time I felt the true emptiness.

I didn't go back to the cemetery until the day I got my drivers license as a seventeen year old. I had been waiting for the moment when I could go to his grave by myself without anyone else knowing or being there with me. I drove to the cemetery and after an hour of searching, I found his grave. I sat there for a long time, just staring at it. It was weird to think that somebody's entire life ends as a slab of stone or as ashes in a vase. I dug my fingernails into the ground, wondering if I dug long enough would I be able to touch his casket, or even better – his bones? Then I realized just how messed up that was and shook myself out of it.

His grave became a source of peace and quiet for me. It was a symbol of who he was, and I wanted to honor it the best way I knew how. I planted seeds, delighted that the next time I went back, they had grown into beautiful flowers surrounding my father's grave. I wrote a poem about it and promptly put it on my MySpace.

It was all I could do.

*

Most young women who become widows try to get 'out there' and date other people, in hopes of a happily ever after that stems from a shitty ending in their first happily ever after. After my father died, my mother was encouraged to try to meet new people and start dating while she 'still had her good looks' but it was extremely difficult to cope and move on from such a tragedy. My mother thought that the love she shared with my father would carry them throughout the rest of their lives and despite everything, it did, until life had other plans.

My mother didn't want to date anybody because she had me to raise, and she knew she would never find anybody as special as my father had been to her. But after constant pushing, she relented and agreed to be taken out on a blind date, matched together by my mother's best friend.

"Mommy, where are you going?" I asked that night, as I watched her put on her makeup.

"I'm going to a comedy show with a friend," she answered, stretching her eyelashes out with a curler. "How do I look?"

"Beautiful," I answered. With blush highlighting her cheekbones and her hair blown out, she really did. She scooped me up and gave me a kiss. The doorbell rang.

I ran to the door before my babysitter could get off the couch and opened it. There was a man standing outside.

I stared at him. "Mommy, there's a guy at the door!" I called out, crossing my arms as he stared back at me nervously.

My mother fixed herself one last time in the mirror and came to meet us at the door. The man looked at my mother and smiled to himself as he observed her beauty. "Okay my love, I'll see you tomorrow morning," she said to me.

"Tomorrow morning?" I asked, lips quivering. It was suddenly clear my mother was going on a date with this man and I didn't like it – at all.

My mother bent down to me. "Yes honey, I'm going out

now. I'll see you when you wake up for school tomorrow because you'll be asleep when I get home."

"Why do you have to go out on a date?" I asked stubbornly.

She paused. She didn't know – she didn't even really want to go. She was doing it, more or less, for everyone else who kept insisting she try to meet someone new, for both of our sakes.

I started to cry. "I want you to stay with me."

"When I come home, I'll wake you up and kiss you goodnight," she assured me, looking pained. I noticed the look on my mother's face and backed off to give her some peace of mind.

As she began to make her way out the door, her date turned around to say goodbye to me. I narrowed my eyes and made a face, hopefully sending the message that if anything happened to my mother, he would pay. I was my mother's protector and I wanted that to be clear. He side eyed me and closed the door behind them.

That night, I couldn't sleep. I waited all night for my mother to come home and once I heard the door creak open, I ran to her, much to my babysitter's embarrassment.

"How was your date, Mommy?" I asked, rubbing my tired eyes.

"Boring," she answered honestly.

I was surprised to hear that. "Why?" I asked.

"It's hard to be somewhere else, when I know I have the world's greatest kid at home." She grinned and I grinned back. "I'd rather be with you."

31

I knew that feeling all too well. My mother and I were a strong team together – and there was no reason to change that. When she would again be encouraged to go out on other dates, my mother would just simply say, "My daughter is the love of my life. She's all I need."

Hometown Glory

I grew up in a brick house right in the middle of Paper Street, the same house that my father and mother rented when they first moved to Meadows years earlier. From the front, passerby would think that there were two big apartments but there were actually four: two small apartments on top, one huge apartment on the first floor lived in by the landlord and his family, and then ours, the tiniest apartment hidden in the back next to a worn-out basketball hoop and a concrete driveway. The luxury of having a basketball hoop was something that I would not overlook, as I would eventually join basketball and be a decent player thanks to practicing at home.

My apartment was so tiny that as a teenager I wondered how we would have survived in such a small place if my father had lived. I would marvel at my friends houses that their parents owned and liked to think that if my father had been alive, he would have eventually built us a big house of our own.

Living in such a small apartment, my mother took pride in keeping it welcoming, decorated warmly, and clean as a whistle. If my mother had to be stuck in what she called a 'shoebox-of-an-apartment', it was going to be inviting – and it was. As soon as you walked through two doors (a chipped, wooden door with cast-iron guards on the peek-window and a white screen door) there was a stand with family pictures in colorful frames that invited you in. Old Norman Rockwell paintings hung in the hallway, leading to a wooden china cabinet full of vintage porcelain china that took up most of the kitchen, given to my mother by her beloved grandmother.

Elongated mirrors in every room made the apartment look bigger than it was, but make no mistake, it was a tiny place to live in. The largest room in the apartment was the master bedroom. No space for laundry, we had our washing machine in the kitchen and it blocked crucial drawers. The living room was small yet full of Springsteen records, Betty Boop figurines, and Elvis Presley memorabilia on a glass TV stand next to my desk, atop of red shag carpets. When my mother got rid of the shag carpets and had brand new tufted carpets installed, every day after school I would come home and vacuum because I loved the look of freshly vacuumed marks on the floor.

Somehow, my mother made the best of a small space because regardless of the size, it was home. Around Christmas time, my mother would put the fake tree we used most of my life on top of a wooden chest in the corner, giving off the false image that the tree was much bigger than it really was. It didn't matter, the presents 'Santa' would bring would fill that entire section of the living room anyway. On many Christmases, the copious amounts of gifts would reach the ceiling – not a small feat for Santa, who was a single mother.

My bedroom was only big enough for a dresser, a bed, and a side table. The walls would eventually be littered with Devon Sawa, Freddie Prinze Jr., and Hanson pictures, ripped out of Big Bopper magazines. I spent time in my bedroom only during daylight hours, because there was a hidden alley behind my window and once teenagers from the block found out about it and started smoking pot back there, I would wake up to their laughing and be too scared to fall back asleep. This ultimately resulted in me sleeping in my mother's bed with her for most of my childhood. I preferred it though – I was safe and so was she.

My block was full of characters but most importantly, Paper Street was full of life. My mother was good friends with several neighbors so when she went over to their houses to drink coffee and chat, I spent a lot of time playing basketball with the boys on my block in the driveway. Our neighbors directly across the street from us had barbeques every summer and while the adults indulged in drinking margaritas, the kids would swim in the pool and drool at the smell of burgers on the grill. My block felt like a town in itself – we were all very much involved with each other – but to everyone else, Paper Street was just a small part of something much bigger: my hometown, Meadows.

*

A small suburban town in New Jersey, Meadows is now home to a diverse mix of people - but when I was growing up, the town was mostly all white families, living in big houses. Meadows was considered a 'safe' place; homeowners left the doors to their homes unlocked, children were able to stay out unsupervised until it got dark outside, and most families were involved in athletic recreation programs. Meadows was a win-win choice when buying a house: low property tax, a short distance from New York City, 45 minutes from the closest beach, great schools, and nature trails. The crime rate in Meadows was unbelievably low, in fact, at the time, the biggest crimes in town were committed by Benny Black.

One of the most infamous (and truest) slogans of Meadows: "You sneeze on the south side of town and everyone already knows about it on the North End." I've heard that quote so many times throughout my life from so many different people, I feel as though it was actually printed somewhere. It's true though, Meadows is so small that people know your business within seconds of it actually happening. If you happened to get into a car accident, your family would arrive at the scene before you even had a chance to contact them because somebody else already did. Loose lips, nosy neighbors, and bored housewives syndrome have fueled the gossip lines for years and years in Meadows.

One year, a member of the local church came to our apartment on Christmas Eve. The doorbell rang and I opened the door to an older woman with a mink coat clutching groceries, potatoes peeking out from the top. As I began to open the screen door, my mother walked up behind me and

36

stopped me, placing her hand against the frame.

"Hello, I am Margaret from the local church," the lady sniffed, her nose runny from the cold outside.

My mother didn't say anything at first, instead she just glanced at the bag of groceries. Finally opening the door, she asked, "How can I help you?"

"Ma'am, this food is from the members of my church."

"Why?" my mother asked, confused.

"Well you see, every year the church collects food during the holiday season for families that may need it. This year we thought you and your daughter could use it," Margaret responded, shifting the groceries in her arms.

My mother's face turned into stone as she cut Margaret short. "Thank you, but the church thought wrong."

"Oh?" Margaret frowned.

"What would make the church think I needed a bag of groceries?"

"Well, we all know about your situation-," she began gently, looking at me.

My mother narrowed her eyes. "Margaret, that's your name, right? Please tell the church that while I do appreciate their kind gesture, I work several jobs to put food on that table," pointing to the kitchen table down the hallway, "and I don't appreciate being treated as if I were a charity case just because my husband passed away."

"Are you sure Ma'am because I-," Margaret started, uncomfortably.

"I am very sure. Now thank you again, I really do appreciate it, but please, go on and deliver that to a family that needs it," my mother replied, smiling sweetly as she closed the door on a very stunned Margaret.

I stared out the door as Margaret walked away in disbelief. "Mom, why'd you do that? She was only trying to be nice."

My mother waved her hand, dismissing it. "They should give that food to somebody who needs it. My cabinets are full. I don't need any handouts. Not to mention, you don't show up on somebody's doorstep with a pity delivery without being asked to. Nobody has ever done that before, nobody should be doing it now. Now they know."

Indeed, they did. We never got another 'pity delivery' again. It was my first lesson on pride.

*

As a single parent, my mother worked several jobs, which sometimes outlasted my school schedule. My mother enrolled me in after school programs, like Sign Language and Arts & Crafts, and it was through these classes that I was introduced to my first real friend.

Sasha, a beautiful little girl complete with brown hair and green eyes, eagerly pushed the door open when my mother and I walked into the Recreation Center. I pulled out one of my Pocket Rockets (little cassette tape players manufactured in the eighties) and showed her. To my surprise, she pulled out her own Pocket Rocket and we immediately began comparing cassette tapes, eventually bonding over a love of Debbie Gibson and Tiffany. For the rest of that visit, we happily played together and cried when it was time to go home.

My mother and her mother became close friends, so from that point on, Sasha and I spent virtually every minute together. We were together so much that one lady asked us if we were sisters while we were food shopping with my mother, which was a common misconception because we were both brunettes. My mother laughed as we looked at each other and giggled. I was about to tell the lady that no, we weren't related, when Sasha grabbed my hand and excitedly said, "Yep! She's the older one!" From then on whenever we were asked, we told everyone that we were sisters because we felt like we were.

Sasha's father was a talented architect who had designed many of the houses on the New York skyline waterfront and her mother was a successful defense lawyer who revolved her life around her practice. Her parents were in the beginning of a nasty divorce while still living together and Sasha and I were witnesses to their brutal arguments plenty of times.

When her parents would scream at each other and things would become volatile, Sasha and I would hide in the basement, pretending we were princesses locked in a dungeon until the screaming died down. Many nights Sasha would be dropped off at my house to sleepover so we could "play", but the real reason was because her parents were embroiled in another heated argument and they knew it wasn't a healthy environment for their daughter.

"You don't know how lucky you are that you don't have to deal with your parents fighting all the time," Sasha would say.

I would look at her with bewilderment and respond back, "You don't know how lucky you are to have both parents around." To the both of us, the grass was greener elsewhere but we were both lucky - and unlucky - in the same sense.

As a result of the impending divorce, Sasha was showered with tons of toys on a regular basis from her parents in hopes to cheer her up – gifts that Sasha would discard as if they were garbage. Sasha was the most spoiled kid I knew but to me, she was also the luckiest. She was given the world handed to her on a silver platter…only for her to throw the platter right back in her parent's faces. The only thing she wanted was for her parents to stay together, which was the one thing she didn't get.

One time, we went to a fundraiser that included hundreds of raffles and since my mother had to work that day, Sasha's mom happily took the both of us. Of course, she spent tons of money to try to win some of the giveaways for the both of us. She switched between writing both of our names on the tickets so that we both had a chance to win something we would like.

As the night went on, it was time to pick the winners. We listened to tons of names being called and were disappointed when ours weren't. For the last giveaway, which was a gift basket full of Barbie's and accessories, we waited in excited anticipation - this was the one raffle Sasha and I both really wanted to win. Magically, my name was called as the winner. I was elated, I had never won anything before and now I had won the Barbie basket!

Sasha fumed. She insisted that since her mother had bought the tickets, the basket should be hers, and that it wasn't fair that I got to keep it. She threw a fit in front of everyone, and even when her mother pointed out that she had a majority of the Barbie's that were in the basket at home already, Sasha was still determined to not go home empty-handed. We ended our night at Toys R Us, her mother spending hundreds of dollars on toys for Sasha, even though once they got home, they ended up in the same corner as the rest of her toys, never to be played with or enjoyed.

*

As we got older, we remained best friends – but on her terms. Sasha was used to getting what she wanted, and if we were going to be best friends, I had to do things her way. She was bossy, controlling, and she loved to order me and everyone else around. A happy-go-lucky (albeit hyper) kid, I was more than happy to keep the peace and follow suit.

A friend of my mother's who worked for a daytime television show asked if I would like to be on TV and if I'd like to bring a friend along. I immediately thought of Sasha, thinking it would be cool to be on TV with my best friend.

The show's segment was based around young girls and what kinds of things girls our age were interested in. That day my mother got my hair done and I wore my finest outfit, a flower-y dress with red glittery shoes (similar to the pair Dorothy had worn in the Wizard of Oz) that I had been saving for a special occasion. I decided to wear them for my TV debut.

We met Sasha and her mother and jumped on the bus going into New York City. I was excited and nervous, but Sasha was suddenly cranky after noticing my outfit. Her mother nervously explained that she hadn't slept well the night before, but I knew she was cranky because she loved the Wizard of Oz and was jealous of my shoes.

Once we entered the TV studio, Sasha's mood went from cranky to unbearable. She copped an attitude with her mother and sniped at the producer, to the point where the producer raised his eyes at my mother and whispered, "This little girl is acting like a bratty child star and she hasn't even been on TV yet."

In the green room before we went on, Sasha crossed her arms and defiantly refused to go on the set and record the show. She screamed and wailed that she didn't want to be on TV anymore. The producers and our mothers pleaded with her to cheer up, but I knew the only thing that would change her mind: giving her the shoes off of my feet.

"Sasha..." I started, as I looked down.

"What?" she asked angrily, sulking.

"Do you want to wear my shoes?" I asked, smiling.

She broke out into a grin and all of a sudden became very pleasant. "Really?" she asked. I bent down, took the shoes off and handed them to her. She reached down, pulled off her shoes and handed them to me without thinking twice, almost as if she had been waiting for me to offer. She had gotten her way, as usual.

"Thanks Ellie," she said, standing up to admire how she

looked now, wearing my magical shoes. We filmed the segment with her wearing my shoes that added a certain mystical appeal to her outfit, and me wearing hers, which clashed with my dress.

It was classic Sasha. She reveled in the fact that I was the un-matched friend, the one who was messy and got in trouble for misbehaving, because she enjoyed playing the role of the one who had her shit together. She was the 'golden child' who behaved sweetly in front of adults while I, the hyper one, became the scapegoat for things that went wrong: "My Nintendo controller broke, it must have been because you were pressing the buttons too hard." "Look at the dirt you just brought in my house, that's what the outside mat is for." In her eyes, whatever the problem was, I was responsible for it.

In Sasha's world, it was her way or no way. If you threatened her with the latter, she would find any way to make things go her way, because if not she would become the world's biggest brat and make things unbearable. I quickly found out it was easier just to follow suit to keep things peaceful and to keep her happy.

This dynamic would be heavily prominent in our friendship for the duration of it, but since she was my best friend and I loved her like how I imagined sisters love their own sisters, I knew no other way than to accept it and deal with it. Besides, Sasha was the first friend of my own to love me for me, regardless of my 'issues'.

Sail

Now, I don't want to make it seem like my childhood was a sob story. It wasn't. Regardless of everything, I had a really fun childhood. I have fond memories of my mother and I watching *Mermaids* and dancing to the last scene when Cher (who plays a single mother in the movie) sings "It's In His Kiss" to her two daughters, played by Winona Ryder and Christina Ricci, while they all wear polka dot dresses with shoulder pads. That movie remains one of my favorites (even if my mother always covered my eyes for the bell tower scene) because I remember looking up to Cher for the single mother she portrayed – and I felt a bit of comfort knowing my mother wasn't the only one.

I began to show signs of having Attention Deficit Disorder in first grade, which at the time, was something mostly only found in boys my age. Young girls were supposed to be sweet, lady-like, and proper, and I was the exact opposite: loud, obnoxious and hyper. My behavior was so wild that the girls in my class were apprehensive of playing with me, forcing me to play more with boys. At that time, my only girl friends were my cousins and Sasha.

At a young age, my mother instilled in me the importance of honesty. As a result, I always told the truth, even when it got me into trouble, which it normally did. One time, my mother made the mistake of calling a girl at my school a 'typical brat' on the phone to someone in front of me.

In all fairness, Lizzie was a brat. Her WASP-y mother, who had married into a wealthy political family, acted as though she were the next coming of Jesus and truly believed her daughter could do no wrong. When her daughter pushed people on the playground or she pulled somebody's hair, it was everybody else's fault. While most parents had no problem disciplining their children in the way they saw fit, this lady refused to even raise her voice to her child, resulting in...you guessed it, a brat.

Our mothers knew each other from high school so the fact that both of their daughters were the same age seemed like an obvious play date choice. My mother, weary of anybody who was pretentious, didn't particularly like this woman because she had become a snob once she had gotten married, but she dealt with her so I had someone else to play with other than Sasha and my cousins.

The four of us set off to use Lizzie's pool one day in the summer. Being a sugar fiend, I was more interested in the delicious fruit snacks we were eagerly awaiting for lunch than actually swimming. Our mothers sternly said that we were not allowed to have the fruit snacks until it was lunchtime, a rule that was more for me because if I had sugar so early in the morning I would be bouncing off the walls.

As our mothers set up their seats and while nobody was looking, Lizzie was stealing fruit snacks from the lunchbox but wouldn't give me any. I reached for one and she slapped my hand away. We began to argue when she pulled my hair. I pulled hers back, except harder, and she started to cry and scream. She was such a wimp.

"What's wrong, sweetness?" her mother cooed, running over to us.

"Ellie pulled my hair!" she cried.

Surprised, my mother and her mother looked at me. My mother wanted an explanation.

"Mom, Lizzie is being a typical brat again!" I said.

Both of their jaws dropped.

"Where did you hear something like that?" her mother asked horrified, looking at my mother, who was trying to hold back an embarrassed laugh.

I pointed at my mother. I was just being honest.

Awkward silence.

By this time, Lizzie was sitting cross-legged on her towel, openly eating a bag of no-longer-restricted fruit snacks, enjoying the trouble she created. She was now grinning.

My mother and her mother stared at each other. I told them what had happened, that I reached out for a fruit snack (that Lizzie had taken out in the first place) and she slapped my hand. She pulled my hair and then I pulled her hair, harder. I crossed my arms. I was satisfied with my explanation because it was, in fact, the truth. How could I get in trouble for telling the truth?

Her mother didn't care, all she cared about was the fact that I must have heard her daughter be called a typical brat somewhere. Not the fact that her daughter had put her hands on me – twice. "Well? How are you going to handle this?" Lizzie's mother asked my mother, swiftly standing up.

It was time to get real. My mother had given her a minute to cool off and after I had just given an honest explanation, that Lizzie didn't even protest to as she happily gobbled fruit snacks, this lady was still pushing her luck.

My mother stood up and declared, "Your daughter should learn to keep her hands to herself."

"How dare you! Elodie is so hyper and wild, how do you know she's not lying?" her mother screeched, obviously not having much of a dignified defense against my mother's statement. What did being hyper have to do with telling the truth?

My mother stopped dead in her tracks so quick, I thought she would tip to the side. Dropping her purse, my mother stuck her face directly into Lizzie's mother's face, nose-to-nose, eerily calm as she said, "Don't talk about my daughter."

I got chills as Lizzie's mother visibly shook. My mother meant business.

"You're barking up the wrong tree. The truth is, Lizzie IS a brat. It's no wonder, seeing as how you are. The mothers at school don't like you and the kids in school don't like your

48

daughter," my mother stated, packing up our stuff and grabbing my hand. "And we don't have time for either one of you."

My mother knew the secret to life that I would find out years and years later: the only way to deal with fake people was to be real with them. So just like that, my partner in crime and I mosey-d off into the sunset, relishing in the fact that although we had less money, we sure as hell had a lot more heart.

*

Having me as a daughter must have been tough. My ADD had rendered me so hyper and overactive, I had to be put into special education classes after first grade because my teachers couldn't handle me anymore. I rode the 'short yellow bus' to school and was in a class with only six other kids. The only time I was calm was when I was reading or writing. I exhausted myself by manically laughing while my mother tried to study my spelling words with me. I, very simply, didn't have the ability to calm down.

You can see on old VHS tapes just how misbehaved I was, me on stage at a school play bothering the girl next to me, despite my mother's embarrassed death-stares in the audience. Me, acting a little too hard, with a cheesy grin while 'making eyes' at the camera, missing my cues and throwing the play off track.

The kids in my special education class had legitimate issues, like a child who had a severe learning disability and another who was autistic. Even though a few of my classmates had frequent outbursts, I didn't consider them different from other kids. I was told quite differently one day when I walked up to an older kid in one of the mainstream classes and asked him if I could play basketball with him and his friends during lunch time. Mainstream classes and special education classes had the same schedule, so we shared our lunch and play time together.

The kid looked at me. "Aren't you in the retard class?"

I didn't know what a retard was, so I shook my head, reaching out for the basketball. He held on to it tightly, shaking his head.

"Do you ride that bus to school?" the kid asked, pointing towards the nearby parking lot where all of the Board of Education buses parked, referring to the small bus in front of all of the big ones.

"Yep, that's my bus!" I said, proudly.

"Yeah, then you must be special," the kid stated, making quotation marks with his fingers.

"Special?" I asked.

"If you ride the short bus, that means you're in the special classes because you're stupid or retarded or something," he said matter-of-factly, as I felt my stomach drop to the floor.

"I'm not st-stupid!" I stuttered, knowing I really wasn't.

"You must be, or you'd be in regular classes with everyone else and not just six other people," the kid said, throwing the basketball over my head to a friend and running away to play, leaving me to pout.

I hid in a corner and cried, angry at the world for making me 'special'. When playtime was over and it was time to go back to class, I watched as classes of twenty students lined up properly as my class lined up a few kids with less ease than the other classes with more kids. As my teacher called my name, I reluctantly walked over with a scowl on my face, embarrassed to be walking alongside of my now-different-to-me peers.

*

After realizing I was considered "stupid" and "special" by the other kids in my school, I started to really act out and behave badly, as opposed to when I used to be just super-hyper. I was now the Tasmanian Devil, looking for attention during school and pushing it away at home. I became fresh to other classmates and boldly challenged my teachers, who were doing everything they could not to strangle me. I began to exhibit some serious behavioral issues.

It was a restless few years. Those years full of parent/teacher conferences, evaluations, therapy sessions and strangers talking over me instead of to me, as if I were a science project that had gone wrong, were sad. I knew something was wrong with me but I didn't know how to fix it – I just thought I was being a kid.

The Child Development Team at my school disagreed. They urged my mother to put me on a new stimulant on the market for children suffering from ADD/ADHD. At first my mother balked at the idea, but after a few sleepless weeks of begging me to study, to take a bath or just to go to sleep, my mother was drained, so she agreed to try it out.

I was off the 'medicine' almost as soon as I was on it. It didn't work properly for me and turned me into a zombie, falling asleep with my head on my textbook in class. Gone was the silly and active girl who made jokes, I was now quiet, sullen and overly tired. My mother yanked me off it, sighing as I began to bounce off the walls again, explaining, "I'd rather have her hyper than medicated." My teacher, reluctantly, agreed.

Later that night, when I was once again manic instead of calm while doing homework, my mother angrily gripped me by the shoulders with desperate tears in her eyes and pleaded with me to start behaving. She couldn't do this anymore. Truth be told, neither could I. I was exhausting myself.

Something about the conversation resonated with me and the next day my mother received a note from my teacher, commending me on my great behavior. I had gone to school, sat in my chair, focused on the lessons and behaved throughout the day. Most importantly, I had kept my mouth shut and not distracted the class with my antics. My mother beamed with pride. I could do this, and now that I knew I could, there was no reason not to.

I literally changed overnight – but it took a lot of understanding that if I ever wanted to be in regular classes with Sasha and other normal kids, I had to maintain that change. I was back in mainstream classes (and more importantly to me, on the regular school bus) by fourth grade. It was a somewhat seamless transition because I genuinely loved school so I was welcomed with open arms. I started to concentrate on reading, writing, and studying and began to bring my grades up. I was a Child Development Team miracle marvel! Here was a kid, who a year ago couldn't sit for more than ten minutes without having to act out, and I was now making Honor Roll. I was focused and concentrated, and I did all of it without needing any medication. It was possible – and I had proved it. I was now one of 'the normal kids' – and nobody was going to take that away from me ever again.

Of course, some would still try.

Sloth's Revenge

Even with all of my friends that I had made at school and outside of school, being an only child was boring once I was back at home. I spent a majority of my time playing by myself. Once I got older, I spent a lot of time at my living room desk reading *The Babysitters Club* and *Sweet Valley High* book series. Those books led me into writing my own stories, using notebook paper, crayons and string to loop the book together through the three holes on the side. All of that time on my own allowed me the ability to become creative.

When writing and reading got boring, I gave myself two imaginary siblings, Brian and Libby. Brian was in high school and would protect me like a big brother was supposed to, and Libby was younger, looking up to me as I was 'the middle child'. Brian would impress us with stories of high school (inspired by Nickelodeon's series *Welcome Back Freshman* and

Fifteen) and he never ceased to amaze me with his imaginary cool life.

My cousins lived in Palisades, in the same town where our mothers had grown up and I spent a lot of time there. Coming from Meadows, which was mostly a safe town and hanging out in Palisades, which was urban, was intimidating. These kids jumped people they didn't like. It wasn't unheard of for my older cousin Bobby to slink into his house with a black eye or wearing only one sneaker because he had gotten jumped in the park.

One morning when I was in seventh grade, my mother and I got into a screaming match. I was going through 'the terrible tween years' and my mother and I weren't seeing eye to eye on a majority of things. The circumstances were stupid but my mother (rightfully so) needed a break from me and my fresh attitude. I came home from school to find my Aunt Maureen and my mother sitting in my living room with my stuff packed into garbage bags, waiting for me.

My Aunt Maureen was the matriarch of our family – she had been the one to raise her siblings when they were kids and she had been the first to have a baby, so being maternal came naturally to her. While she was loving, she was also strict, strict, strict – way stricter than my mother. Hell, I had it easy compared to my cousins. My aunt didn't take shit from anybody, especially children, and when you walked in her house, you walked in with respect or else.

I was intimidated by my aunt so I screamed, argued, and begged – but at the end of it all, I had no choice but to crawl to her car and stay at her house for a week to be taught various lessons, one that included cleaning a shower with a toothbrush.

I never realized how spoiled I was while living with my mother, but I got a good dose of reality while living at my aunt's. My cousins had to clean up after themselves, do their own laundry, and had a chore list that made my eyes water. It was torture for me, seven days of hell, but it was routine for them. My aunt would call my mother shocked, *"Elodie doesn't know how to wash dishes?"*

My aunt cooked differently than my mother and I couldn't handle the variety. I am a notoriously picky eater. I don't eat meat and they lived off it. I don't like tomatoes and there were huge pieces in all of the sauces. Even worse, my cousins...actually...had...to...eat...vegetables. As I sulked every night at the table for dinner, my cousins would finish their meal, wash their plates and retreat outside to play with neighbors while I would be stuck at the table until it was bedtime. If I didn't eat, I didn't play, so I just cried.

That Saturday, while hanging out with my cousin's friends from the block, there was a fight over my brand new pink bike with glittery streamers that came out of the handlebars. This girl Billie wanted to ride it, but my mother had told me not to let anyone use it out of fear of it being broken, so I said no. For whatever reason, Billie punched me in the face and gave me a black eye.

At the time, I had never been punched before and I was stunned, not knowing how to react. In Palisades, if you hit somebody, you're getting into a real fistfight and somebody is going to get hurt. I was a coward at this time, so I backed up, falling into the corner. The daughter of my mother in me told me to punch her back but reality insisted, "Get your ass out of there before you get jumped." So I ran. Fast.

I ran back to my aunt's house a few blocks away. I tripped on my way into the door, that's how scared-fast I was running. My mother, who was visiting to check in on me, my aunt, and my cousins were waiting for me. As soon as they saw my black eye, they immediately went into battle-mode.

"Elodie, what happened!?" my aunt nervously shrieked.

"This girl Billie punched me in the face because she wanted to ride my bike and I said no and she cornered me," I began, out of breath.

"DID YOU HIT HER BACK? YOU BETTER HAVE HIT HER BACK!" Bobby shouted.

"IF YOU ARE BACKED INTO A CORNER, YOU FIGHT YOUR WAY OUT!" my mother screamed, throwing up her hands.

"I was scared!" I started to whimper. Most parents would be relieved that their kid hadn't hit back, but not my mother. She hadn't raised her daughter to be a pushover just like she hadn't been raised to be one.

Bobby started for the door. "Where are you going, Bobby? We don't want any problems!" my Aunt Maureen pleaded. He continued for the door, slamming it behind him as we all rushed to watch.

Billie and her group of friends were now across the street at a mutual friends house. Bobby stalked towards them, grabbing Billie's worn out bike and shoving it down the street until it hit a car and smashed the window, breaking the handlebars. Everyone just stared. That was a little much even by their standards.

"If you ever touch my cousin again, that'll be YOU going through a window," my cousin said, pointing directly in Billie's face, motioning towards the broken shards on the ground. Knowing he meant it, she ran away quicker than I had ran fifteen minutes earlier. I never had problems with her ever again...or anyone else in Palisades, for that matter.

It was the first time a male had stood up for me – and at that young age I knew enough to appreciate and respect Bobby for putting himself out there when he could have very easily ended up getting beat up for it. He did it anyway. He had a sister of his own to protect but he still had my back because we were blood. He made me feel safe and that made me feel good.

It was more than my imaginary brother Brian would ever do. After that, I said goodbye to my imaginary creations and rested knowing that I may not have had an older brother to look out for me, but I had a cousin who would.

*

Billie from Palisades marks the beginning of the my-being-bullied days. That same year, I was walking to a park with Sasha and we came across three older eighth graders who were a little advanced for their age. They rocked big hoop earrings, dark lip-liner, and baggy jeans accompanied by baby doll shirts that didn't pass their pieced navels. They were 'the hood girls' of our middle school, aka the scary chicks, and the ones no girl wants to have problems with because they'd kick ass without hesitation.

They walked past us and one of them started calling us names. I was holding a bottle of Pepsi in my hand and I surprised myself as I watched my hand rise up and lunge it towards the girl's mouth. It connected, almost splitting her lip in half. 'Oh shit,' I thought to myself, 'Did I really just do that?' I had. I was screwed and I knew it.

Almost immediately they lunged for me, one of them hooking me right in the nose. I was bleeding and about to get my ass handed to me. They hit me a couple of extra times and after realizing that I didn't know how to fight back, they got bored and eventually walked away, leaving me bleeding and Sasha embarrassed.

I pathetically walked home to run into my mother coming home from work. She immediately became irate. "YOU NEED TO START DEFENDING YOURSELF, ELODIE! WHO DID THIS TO YOU?" she screamed.

When my mother used my full name, I knew she was serious so I told her through tears. She blasted through the door and jumped in her car, finding the girls down the block from our house. My mother got into their faces and threatened them, cornering them. Charges were almost pressed – until the next day in school when the girl who had originally called me names walked up to me, apologizing.

At first I was scared because I didn't really want to get my ass kicked again, especially in the middle of the hall where everyone from my school would be a witness, so I backed away.

"No, no, don't be scared. I wanted to say I'm sorry," she

said cautiously.

"Why the sudden change of mind?" I asked, still unsure.

"I shouldn't have hit you." She paused. I stared at her, confused. "Um, the truth is, my mom really doesn't want problems with your mom. She went to high school with her... and she's like, really scared of her," she sighed, embarrassed to admit it.

Here was one of the most feared chicks in my middle school and she was apologizing to me. At that moment, I realized the impact of being my mother's daughter. I silently thanked God at that moment for giving me my fierce mom, even if he had taken my father away too.

Whatever reputation preceded my mother, people knew better than to mess with her and hopefully that would trickle down to me so I didn't have to worry about being bullied all the time. *(Not quite.)* Still, at least they would know there would be consequences. It would become clear throughout my life that people feared my mother - with good reason – but they also respected her.

That was good enough for me.

*

In eighth grade, I quit playing basketball for the year, telling my mother I needed a break from the constant practices and weekend games. I become lazy and spend most of my afternoons binge eating and watching *Sally Jessy Raphael* on my couch while my mother is at work. As a result, I lost my semi athletic body while gaining weight that at my heaviest, formed into an unattractive flabby belly that pops through shirts, highlighting my belly button. I had been chubby before, but now I am fat.

I now spend a majority of my time hanging out with my new friend Maggie, who is considered eccentric. She listens to punk music, hates the popular kids and dyes her hair exotic colors, anarchy signs drawn on her notebooks. Maggie and I become best friends. We are different from the rest of the girls in our grade, but because we know this, we have no reason to try to impress anybody. We ended up spending so much time together that people joke that we must be lesbians.

Kyle Hall, a snotty senior, calls me "Ellie Belly" one day as I walk past him and his friends erupt in laughter because apparently the nickname fits. "Ellie Belly" sticks and suddenly all of the seniors begin to torment me everyday in school pointing out my chubbiness. Everyday, without fail, whether I am walking to class or to lunch, I pass by someone who calls me names that make my heart drop.

I tried to not pay much attention but it became so torturous that I couldn't even grab my usual snack between classes without coming across some asshole that felt the need to make fun of me. It got so bad that I refused to go out for Freshmen Friday, a night where the seniors take out the upcoming freshman to get drunk and 'bond', because I knew the entire night would be full of jokes about my weight. I couldn't bear to be humiliated and not be able to defend myself, so I stayed home with Maggie while the rest of our grade was initiated into becoming 'cool'.

Kyle took a personal liking to tormenting me and would

go far and beyond, even more so outside of school. The local diner was a hotspot in Meadows and everyone would gather there after a long night to replenish themselves with greasy cheese fries and burgers. Kyle's disgusting bullying was put on display when an obese woman walked into the diner and because she was so thick, she got stuck walking between the booths. Kyle cupped his hands around his mouth and yelled, "Ellie Belly in a few years!" I was mortified, as I was sitting in a booth behind him and when Maggie looked at me in horror, I ran into the bathroom sobbing, only coming out to go home.

That night when I got home, for the first time ever, I considered becoming anorexic, but I knew that I couldn't avoid eating – I loved food too much. I stared at myself in the bathroom mirror, grabbing my belly with both hands and cried. I couldn't handle being bullied any longer.

My cries eventually became louder and my mother knocked on the door asking if something was wrong. I cried back, "I'm fine, ma!" My mother, never one to take 'no' for an answer, opened the door and welcomed herself into the bathroom.

A look of devastation grew slowly when she saw my swollen, beat red and tear-stained face and asked what happened. When I told her what I had been dealing with at school and the events of that night, she surprisingly ran her fingers through my hair calmly and smiled. I became angry, what was there to smile about?

My mother explained, "The boys that make fun of you now will be kissing the ground you walk on one day." This advice pissed me off even more so I begged her to leave my room and she obliged, saying, "You'll see. One day you'll come to me and tell me I was right!" I rolled my eyes and slammed my door after her, and promptly cried myself to sleep.

*

At this point, I was sick of crying over seniors that were graduating that year, most of whom I hoped to never see again. I was giving them the ability to torment me because I wouldn't stick up for myself. I vowed to myself that the night at the diner was the last time that would ever happen again.

At lunch two days later, one of Kyle's friends, Tony, sat down at our table. Tony just so happened to be dating Sasha (a senior dating an 8th grader, what a winner, right?) and most lunch periods I would pray he was in a good mood so he would leave me alone so I could eat in peace. He had a smug look on his face as he positioned himself in his seat and crossed his arms over his chest. I sensed a bad vibe and felt uncomfortable with the snide look he was giving me. Staring back at him, I slowly mirrored his position, leaning back on the chair with my arms crossed over my chest.

We made eye contact. I waited. Words were exchanged and somehow, he made an "Ellie Belly" comment. It felt like someone had ripped the tab off a grenade in my stomach. As soon as he muttered those two evil words, adrenaline and rage began to run into my blood and from there on out, I was no longer accountable for my reaction. I popped up out of my seat, slamming my hands on the table, knocking over everyone's lunch. Ignoring my friends whining about their

Snapple ice tea spilling onto their jeans, I lost it. "WHAT THE HELL IS YOUR PROBLEM?" I snapped.

The entire lunchroom went silent and steadied their focus on me. Tony's face went white and he couldn't even muster a response. "Why does making me feel bad about myself make you feel good?" I accused, loudly. "I mean, how distorted is that?"

Tony kept quiet, embarrassed because the entire lunchroom was watching him get bitched out by an eighth grader. The silence was so deafening, someone dropped something on the floor and other than my screaming, that was the only noise heard by everyone. I expected Tony to get up and go word for word with me, but he still said nothing. He looked sympathetic, like he felt bad, but that wasn't enough.

I continued, "I've had it with being bullied for my weight! If I want to be the world's fattest teenager, that's my business, not yours! So knock it off!"

Instantly, whispers started to fill the air. My demeanor proved I wasn't kidding. Seeing the anger and hurt in my eyes, Tony cleared his throat and said, "Listen, I was just kidding, my bad. I'll stop. I promise. I'll tell everyone else too."

Clenching my jaw, I shook my head and looked around to all the faces staring at me. Some people probably thought I was crazy to cause such a scene but others seemed impressed by how I was finally defending myself. They, deep down, felt bad for me every time they had to walk past me, hearing the name calling as tears filled my eyes – even if they didn't defend me in the meantime. I couldn't blame them though, why defend somebody and put yourself in the crossfire? It was easiest to just keep quiet.

I decided to use this opportunity and spoke loudly so everyone would hear me, "I'm going to make you eat those words. That's a promise. I'll lose this weight but you'll always be an asshole."

With that being said, I took my seat and continued to eat my lunch. The girls at my table all looked at each other out of the corners of their eyes and quietly continued on with their lunch as Tony got up from the table and left. I knew he would pass the word along.

*

If I wanted Kyle and Co. to stop teasing me, I had to eliminate the reason they were. To me, that meant losing weight and getting skinny again. If I lost weight, their name-calling wouldn't hurt me anymore. Eager to see results, I started exercising that night and I began to eat healthy, turning down my mothers infamous chicken cutlets and mashed potatoes that I basically lived for, to eat bland salads. I started practicing basketball again in preparation for my freshman year in high school, hoping I would make varsity. My hard work paid off: I went from 150lbs to 130lbs (showing obvious progress on my 5'5 frame) by the end of the year, which was thankfully also the same time the seniors were graduating.

My last day of being an eighth grader, and twenty pounds lighter, I strutted down the hall confidently because I knew that this was the last time I would have to deal with the seniors who were graduating. I saw Kyle and Tony standing by their lockers and I no longer felt that usual pit in my stomach. I walked past them and saw Kyle's mouth start to open. Tony noticed, hit him in his ribs and shook his head. I put my locker combination in and slowly opened the locker, waiting for Kyle to make a wise-ass remark. He didn't.

Tony walks over, puts his arm around me and says, "I respect you, kid. Good luck in high school."

"Peace!" I said cheerily, shrugging his arm off of mine. I walked away, dignity in tact, and now, bully-bullshit free.

You Always Say Goodnight

Freshman year, I am still best friends with Sasha and Maggie. During lunch, we sit with a group of girls who aren't exactly popular, but who aren't exactly not popular: they waver in the middle. I am not so sure where I belong. During this time, I am a bit awkward, growing into myself and I have absolutely no flirting genes. This makes it impossible for me to land the hot guys in my grade, but I am too confident for the weird ones. Therefore, while the rest of my friends are losing their virginities, I haven't even been kissed yet. Fine by me, because I want my first kiss to be special.

As it turns out, it would be.

One of my friends at the lunch table, Molly, is dating a junior named Ryder. A good-looking kid who doesn't give a shit about anybody but himself, Molly and Ryder will clash in more ways than one throughout their volatile relationship. He is a popular, well-known kid in school and he has a ton of guy friends who plop their asses down at our lunch table and take it over as if it was theirs. The girls and I don't mind because it makes us look cool that a bunch of mediocre freshmen are sitting with juniors, even if we did have to eat our lunches cramped.

Out of all of Ryder's friends, one strolls over, and upon resting his sight on my face, chooses to sit in the chair right next to me.

His name is Sam.

I had seen Sam in the halls before, walking confidently to class. The year prior I had witnessed him sit at a lunch table with a new kid in school who hadn't made any friends yet and was sitting alone. Most high-schoolers would see a person sitting alone and either think nothing of it or judge them, but Sam was kinder than everyone else, and he promptly sat with him for a few weeks until the kid agreed to sit at Sam's original table to get to know his friends.

Sam asks me what I'm eating and I make a face before asking, "You don't know what a salad is?" He laughs and we begin small talk. After hearing that I am very much into music, he tells me I should listen to q104.3, a NYC classic rock radio station.

"Q104.3? Isn't that, like, for old people?" I joke.

He winces, as if the mere question wounded him. "No, no. They play classics. They play the kind of music that all those garbage bands on the radio today wish they had thought of first. Put it on the next time you're near a radio." I nodded and said I would, making a silent note in my head.

Sam decides to make his 'official seat' the one next to mine, when he could have sat anywhere else. He wants to be next to me so we can chat about music – and I don't mind it. As a result, every day I look forward to lunch. During class breaks, I seek him out in the hall, lingering a little longer than normal in hopes he'll stop by and chat.

He asks for my phone number one day while we are eating lunch. I don't expect him to call, especially since he had just broken up with a pretty senior who just so happened to be the class president, editor of the school newspaper, and the type of popular senior every freshman wishes to be. She has hard shoes to fill and I'm not so sure I could ever do it. Actually…I know I can't.

One night I am getting home from junior varsity basketball practice and he calls. I am surprised to hear his voice on the other side of the phone, but I am more excited than anything. I call him back after my shower and we talk for hours, way past the time that my mother comes into my room and orders me to hang up because it's time to go to sleep. I wait until she leaves, hiding the phone, and promptly get back on the line as soon as she's out of eyesight.

He tells me to put on the radio and tune into q104.3, so we can listen to the station together, just at different houses and over the phone. Sam begins to educate me on the stories behind the songs, "Did you know Carly Simon's song "Vain" is supposedly about Warren Beatty?"

"Who?" I ask.

"That actor."

"Oh yeah…" I answer, having no idea who that is.

"Do you not know who I'm talking about?" he teases, sensing the confusion in my voice.

"Nope," I admit.

He laughs, responding, "You're funny. He played Dick Tracy." I blush when he calls me funny and I realize this is the first guy that has ever flirted with me.

I am intrigued by his passion in music and he's pleased when he realizes I know most of the songs on the radio. He is impressed that I know more than the average teenager when it comes to Bruce Springsteen and I surprise him when I tell him that I secretly listen to my father's old Bay City Rollers albums to feel close to him. He tells me that he does the same thing to feel close to his own father who had passed years earlier. It is comforting finally knowing somebody else who feels the heaviness of a father's absence like I know so well. I have found someone who 'gets it'.

Lynrd Skynrd's "Sweet Home Alabama" comes on the radio and he tells me that they are his favorite band, as he begins to pour out more impressive trivia. "This song was written for Neil Young because he released two songs that talked shit on Alabama. They actually name him in the song. It was like Tupac and Biggie beef, just a Southern version - and not as violent."

The song is over, and since it is Two-For-Tuesday, q.104 plays two songs from the same band back to back. The next song, "Freebird", is a song I had never heard before, but Sam says excitedly, "This is my favorite song, ever!"

"This is your favorite song? Isn't it a little depressing?" I ask after listening for a moment.

"No, no. It's a beautiful song. It's only depressing if you let it be. Just listen." We continue to listen as I play with the phone cord between my fingers. "Get it? He's telling someone he loves that he has to go explore other worlds. He's got to fly away and be a free bird. I like the idea of that."

I knew what he meant. "That's deep," I say. He laughs.

I hear my mother stirring in the other room and I know I am mere seconds from getting caught being on the phone. He calls me a 'grandma' for having to hang up.

"Shut up. I'll see you at school tomorrow," I say, grinning into the phone.

"Yes. You. Will. Goodnight," he tells me confidently, hanging up. Out of sheer excitement, I struggle to fall asleep.

From then on we talk on the phone every night and we begin to grow very close. He introduces me to underrated music of indie bands that I've never heard of, like the Get Up Kids. He discusses his ex-girlfriend, and I talk about frivolous things, not having any past relationships to complain about. He becomes not just a random acquaintance who sits at my lunch table, but a friend, a confidant. It's nice knowing a guy who cares about me, who I trust on the same level as my girl friends.

One morning, while hanging out by our lockers before class, Ryder lets me in on a secret. "I think Sam likes you." My stomach and heart burst into butterflies as I begin to ask the kind of questions that you would expect a fourteen year old to

73

ask: "Why do you think that?" "What did he say?" "Did he say anything else?" "Yeah, but how did he sound when he said it?" Clearly, I like him too.

That day at lunch, I am nervous around him now that I suspect he likes me. This is new territory to me. I avoid his gaze, I ignore his routine questions, and engage in conversation with my other friends longer than I normally would. As the bell rings, letting us know that lunch is over, I grab my things and hurry to my class. He follows me, keeping up with every step I take.

"Why are you being weird?" he accuses.

"I'm not! Let's talk later," I hastily answer as I make a sharp turn into my class and leave him behind the closing door. I see a look of disappointment on his face as I sit in my seat, with him still looking inside the classroom at me. He shakes his head and retreats to his own class.

'That was stupid,' I think to myself. 'What kind of idiot shuts out the person they like because that person actually likes them back?' The truth is, I am so uncomfortable in my own skin that it seems almost impossible that he would have feelings for me. I begin to reason with myself, 'If he didn't like me, he wouldn't call me everyday. He definitely wouldn't choose to sit next to me during lunch when he can sit next to anyone. Maybe he does like me...'

I wasn't ugly - but I was an athletic tomboy. I also had slight post traumatic stress disorder caused by the remnants of the Ellie Belly year. I didn't know how to work with what I had and up until then, I hadn't really cared enough to try. I fought the always-present thought in my brain, 'What self-respecting

74

junior would admit to having a crush on the girl formally known as Ellie Belly?'

He called that night, and I acted as though nothing had changed. We both went along with it and resumed our normal nightly chat.

*

In February, the SGO arranges a 'send a valentine' candy gram system where you buy a little valentine card with a lollipop attached to it. You pay $5, write your message on the card, and have it delivered to your valentine during first period. Girls would squeal with delight, not only for getting a valentine, but also for having somebody come into their class and announce that they were desired and loved in front of everyone. All of the pretty, popular girls get tons of lollipops while the not-so-cool chicks just stare ahead, hoping not to catch anyone's pity stare that they hadn't received a candy gram.

I couldn't care less. This period was actually my favorite class, English Literature with my favorite teacher, so when the SGO president gently knocked on our door to deliver the valentines, I was more annoyed that he was interrupting a great discussion on The Great Gatsby. I rolled my eyes as my teacher opened the door and he galloped in.

"Candy-grams are in!" The SGO president bellowed. "Let's see, I have one for Mackenzie, one for Annie..." I hang my head as he continues, writing in my notebook, hoping to take this interruption as an opportunity to jot down significant things my teacher has mentioned in regards to Friday's test. "...And two for Ellie," he finished, looking at me.

Everybody's heads whip towards me with their eyes wide. My peers are surprised, but not as much as me. I try to read the SGO President's face to see if this is a joke, but as he walks toward me holding out two candy-grams, I know he is being serious. One is one thing, but two?

My hands slightly tremble as I receive the candy grams. I notice my cheeks get flushed as everyone stares and I realize that for somebody who likes to be the center of attention, I sure as hell don't like it when it happens without me asking for it. I open the candy gram.

It's from Sam and his best friend Jordan, another friend who sits at our lunch table with Ryder and the guys. I smile to myself. They were doing the gentlemanly thing and must have sent all of the girls at the lunch table one. I set it down, ripped the lollipop out and began to suck on it. Noticing that my teacher was ready to resume the lesson, I quickly snuck a look at the other one and opened it slowly.

This one is from Sam, by himself:

Ellie,
You are so pretty.
Will you be my valentine?
- Sam.

I almost choke on my lollipop. Pretty? Valentine?

Later in the day before lunch, I run into Sam and he is walking through the halls with Jordan. I am shy, not knowing whether or not Jordan knows Sam had sent me a private candy gram. "Did you get our candy gram?" Jordan asks, high-fiving me.

I jump up to slap his hand. "Yes, thank you so much! That was nice of you guys." He nods triumphantly, and walks away, leaving Sam and I to chat.

"Well....?" Sam asks.

"Well what?" I deadpan, not letting in on the joke.

His face falls. "Didn't you get mine too?"

I hit his arm playfully. "Yes. Thank you." I blush, embarrassed by the moment. We don't address the Valentine question. He nods, walking away and leaving us both off to wonder.

*

That night he doesn't call. I curse myself out for being such a weirdo as I wait for a phone call that never comes. Disappointed, I log onto AOL to see if he is online. He isn't, but I am relieved to see an email from him in my inbox.

Subj: hey

whats up nothing much here sorry I didn't call tonight I knew u had basketball practice and I was setting up for the valentines dance and I just got home anyway what are we doing for valentines day screw the dance id like to take u out to eat or something like that I don't know we'll make it fun do u wanna chill or something?

beep me if u do

oh ive been in such a bad mood the last couple of weeks but for some reason I cant get u out of my head and ur making it better thanks so much well im going to go ill see u tomorrow

PS u looked good today, real good...

i would have told u that in person but u probably wouldn't have let me anyway, right?

goodnight Ellie

Take On Me

For so long, I couldn't be convinced that Sam liked me. I considered myself unpretty, undateable, and undesirable since enduring the Ellie Belly years. I had seen enough tortured high school chick flicks to know that in every school there was at least one laughingstock and I assumed that for Meadows High School, I held that title.

Even after countless conversations and numerous attempts, I kept my wall up, in an attempt to protect myself but also to protect Sam. He could do much better than me and already had. He was considered a cool kid, and I didn't think he should sabotage his well-standing reputation for dating a former fat girl. I cared enough about him that I wouldn't allow it.

Sam grew frustrated. He didn't understand how anybody could feel so negatively about themselves especially since he saw something in me that I didn't see myself. He was a positive person, the kind of person who walked past flowers and actually stopped to smell them. He didn't care if anybody liked him because he liked himself enough to not worry about other people's opinions, which was rare in high school. I admired that about him.

"I'm not good enough for you," I would always say, explaining why I wasn't pretty enough, thin enough, or popular enough. In a school run off of hormones and hook-ups, I didn't think a guy would proudly admit to liking me. The social climate of Meadows High School was like a warzone and it seemed wise to be on the bandwagon then to be one of the people creating waves, being different.

"I can't believe you really feel that way about yourself, Ellie," he would say, shaking his head with genuine sadness, while trying to convince me otherwise.

After an exhausting all-night conversation on why I turned him down to taking me out for Valentines Day, he sauntered into the food court at the Meadows Mall, where we all went after school to hang out. Instead of plopping down next to me, he stood on top of his chair. Our friends looked at him like he had three heads. What the hell was he doing, making an announcement? He cleared his throat.

"I like this girl. I like her a lot," Sam declared loudly, pointing to me, now horrified, slouching in my seat. "I like every single thing about her and I don't really give a damn what anybody else thinks. I just wanted to let you all know that."

Everyone looks at him, then looks at me, and with expressions of being unimpressed, continue on with their lunch, discussing what stores to blow money in once they were done eating.

I grab his shoulder, pulling him down, "Are you crazy? Why'd you do that? That was so embarrassing!"

"Do you believe me now?" he pressed. I stared at him baffled. Did this kid really just scream from the rooftops that he liked me?

Suddenly, I felt something.

It was happiness.

"We can be something special, if you let it happen," he winked. "I promise."

I believed him…so I decided that I would.

*

That weekend, we all went to Third Street Park, a dead-end park on the south part of town where very few people go at night. Bored, Ryder casually offered up playing a game of truth or dare. We all sat in a circle, some of us sitting on swings while the others sat on foam tiles, and eager to spice up our night, we agreed to play. Ryder went first and we dared him to kiss his girlfriend, Molly. Simple.

On the second turn, since I was sitting next to Ryder, it was my turn to go. My friends exchanged mischievous glances as Ryder cleared his throat. "So, truth or dare?"

"Truth," I said, laughing. I wasn't stupid. Who knew what this kid would dare me to do? I sure as hell wasn't going to jump off any buildings or eat any bugs.

"Nope."

"No?" I asked.

"No, you're going to do a dare. I dare you to have your first kiss…right now…with Sam," Ryder said.

So that's what all of those glances meant.

Instantly, butterflies let loose in my stomach. I looked at Sam. He was already standing up, making the hand motion towards Ryder's truck, silently urging me to come. He extended his hand down to me. I looked at Maggie, Molly, and Sasha who were giving me intense 'GO' faces and I knew I had no choice. I stood up and took his hand. I took a deep breath and followed behind him. He opened the door for me, gestured in and said, "Ladies first." He was always such a gentleman, I couldn't help but grin. With that, I exhaled, blushed, and got in.

We climbed into the backseat and he reached over to the front to put the radio on, satisfied when he found q104.3. "Every Little Thing She Does Is Magic" by The Police was playing and he rests back, content with the mood music.

"So…," he said, popping a piece of Winterfresh in his mouth.

"So…," I say, grabbing a piece.

"You ready?" he asks, studying my face.

"No," I say carefully, "I'm nervous."

"How can you still be nervous with me?" he asked, annoyed. He was right, we had spent way too much time together for me to be shy about this now.

"I've never kissed anyone before."

He knows this already. "That's why I plan on making your first kiss special."

I smile, knowing this to be the truth.

He takes my smile as a sign and surprises me by grabbing my face, enclosing his lips on my lips and gently slipping his tongue in my mouth. We begin to kiss. He is gentle, my kissing teacher, and I am willing and eager to learn. We spend the rest of our time dancing around each other's mouths as he runs his hands through my hair, tugging at all the right spots. I enjoy my first real kiss as Sting sings on about magic and the scent of cool Winterfresh gum fills the air.

*

The next night, Ryder, Sam and Molly picked me up in Ryder's truck for a double date. Sam had just gotten his driver's license so he was overjoyed when Ryder told him he could drive. I sat in the front seat next to him and we held hands. We drove through the back roads of Meadows, listening to The Who, and explored parts of town that I had never seen before. Finding a spot by deserted train tracks next to a river than ran through Meadows, Sam parks the truck. Ryder and Molly get out to walk along the water, leaving us alone.

The album continues to play and "Baba O'Reilly" comes on. Thinking of the night before when I had my first kiss, I looked at him, surprised to see him already staring at me. He touches my face, pulls me in, and we kiss fast and furiously to the increasing adrenaline-packed chorus playing in the background, almost as if our heartbeats were embedded in the song.

Sam and I start dating, officially. When we aren't together, we spend time on the phone or talking online, with him dedicating songs to me that I promptly post onto my AOL profile. We write each other long notes, folded into triangles, that we pass each other every day at lunch. I meet his family and he meets my mother, and we are both welcomed warmly.

For someone who had never been kissed before, I make up for lost time by making out with Sam every chance I get. We skip lunch and kiss behind the stairs until the bell rings, with me running to class, fixing my lip-gloss and him going to class with a Cheshire cat grin on his face. We both begin to take so many bathroom breaks to meet up during our classes that my math teacher asks me if I have a "problem" and if I did, I should see the nurse. We eventually get caught kissing by the principal and are scolded on what type of behavior is appropriate while in school. Apparently, making out on school property isn't, so we both serve detention – separately.

One day, instead of our usual pass-the-note session in between classes, he stops me outside his class.

"I have to show you something!" he says, obviously excited.

"What?!" Seeing him so excited has me excited.

He leads me to the nearest window. He points out towards the parking lot, where the seniors and juniors parked their cars.

I squint my eyes. "What am I looking at?"

"See that car in the third spot?" he asks. I nod.

84

"That's mine! I got a car!" he exclaimed.

I jumped up and down, clapping my hands, grinning ear to ear. I knew that Sam having his own car meant more time for us.

"Pick you up tonight around eight? Let's cruise," he suggests, already knowing my answer.

"See you then!" I kiss him on the lips and squeeze his hand.

I wait all day for 8pm and in true Sam fashion, he arrives early at 7:45 to pick me up. He reaches over the passenger side to let me in and as I get in the car, I am appreciative that I have a boyfriend who happens to have his own car now too. No more relying on friends, we would be able to do our own thing from there on out.

As I get in and check out his new car, he smiles, and takes my hand as I rest in the passenger seat, eagerly taking in the smell of his Aqua De Geo cologne. I put on the radio so we can indulge in our favorite music and I laugh when I realize he hasn't bothered to pre-set any music stations other than q104.3.

Sam drives through the back roads of Meadows once again, parking at the same spot that we had been at with Ryder and Molly, and he lowers the music. "Shall we get out?" he asks, looking out the window towards the sky. I tell him sure and he grabs a blanket from his backseat and puts it on top of his hood so we can lie out on it.

We share a peaceful silence while stargazing. It's a rare clear night in New Jersey and the sky seems almost transparent. "Look at how bright those stars shine!" I muse.

"You shine, Shine," Sam tells me, proclaiming that as

my new nickname while turning his head towards me. He makes me feel that way. I rest my head on his shoulder, and knowing he really believes what he has said, I kiss him harder, more passionate than I've ever kissed him before.

We enjoy the stars.

*

Over the course of the rest of that school year and the following summer, Sam and I embark on many adventures and share many beautiful memories. We go to the library and read books while sitting next to each other in comfortable silence. We listen to tons of music while taking car rides to nowhere in particular in his car. We take walks, we smell flowers, and we stargaze.

Sam surprises me the last weekend before school started again, when Sasha and Maggie throw me an impromptu birthday party in Sasha's basement while her parents are away on vacation. Sam had gotten in trouble and was grounded indefinitely. All day I had been sulking, pissed off at Sam for getting grounded, and disappointed because here I was having a party thrown in my honor, and all I wanted to do was be with him.

As soon as I got to Sasha's house (I was running late over a wardrobe malfunction) I opened the door and all eyes fell on me. "What?" I asked, apprehensive of the sudden staring, wondering if my outfit looked bad.

Suddenly Sam appeared from hiding behind the door

with a red bow on his head, holding a birthday cake. Everyone had been in on the secret of him asking his parents for a get-out-of-being-grounded-free pass because it was my birthday and them saying okay. I was elated and we begin what was to be, a very successful birthday party.

Over the course of the night, I drink alcohol for the first time ever and get drunk. I ask him to come outside with me and he does, taking my hand as we walk. It's becoming chilly out, so he brings me into his chest, sharing his jacket. We hold each other tight as he squeezes me and says, "I love you." I shiver from the cold, but also from hearing those words come from a guy that I love back. I tell him that I love him too, and we kiss, ignoring the crisp incoming fall wind brushing past our faces.

*

What I love most about Sam is that he is confident and honestly doesn't give a damn about what anybody else thinks. He sees through the jokes and sees to me, to my heart, to my soul, to the person I can be when given the opportunity to feel as though I have self worth. "Stop worrying about what other people think about you," he tells me. "The only thing that matters is how you feel about yourself."

As a result, he gives self worth to me. He gives me confidence. He treats me with respect, holds the car door open for me, and embraces me as though I was a pretty girl, just like the others. For the second time in my life, I feel normal. I am just like everybody else. Somebody loves me.

That first year with him, my first love, educated me in ways that are so profound, there's no way to express it properly. I know this because I've tried…and failed.

Kryptonite

After some time of heavenly bliss with Sam, our relationship shifts. In September, after our awesome summer together, I go into the new school year as a sophomore and he, a senior. We attend the Pep Rally together, as I watch in pretend horror at his goofy rendition of "Material Girl" on stage in front of half our town. As he sings the words to the song, he points directly at me and pretends to sing to me. I blush as everyone looks in my direction, curious of this public display of adoration. Sam wins everybody over after the Pep Rally and he becomes suddenly popular overnight.

He ends up running for Class President because he loses a bet with a jock, and he actually wins, catapulting himself as one of the cool kids. It was inevitable though, Sam was too charismatic to be overlooked and he deserved all of the attention he got.

It wasn't only that he was 'too cool' for me once all of

these fun things started happening in his life, but I also started being 'not cool' with all the girls who were suddenly paying more attention to him now that he was on their radar. I noticed girls in his grade who had never looked at him twice before, suddenly checking him out, regardless of me eye-balling them the entire time. Knowing an inexperienced sophomore couldn't compare to wild seniors, I felt a sense of insecurity I hadn't felt since the Ellie Belly days. Sam had respected my decision to stay a virgin, but I knew those days were going to end at some point.

Sam started distancing himself from our mutual friends and started hanging out more with the popular kids, leaving our group of friends to consider him a poser. We had been the ones to love him before he was 'in', and now he was dropping us to kiss the asses of people we used to laugh at? It hurt all of us, but it hurt me the most.

He developed an ego. Who could go back to the innocent days of going to the mall, driving around, and stargazing with me when he now knew how much fun hanging out with the 'in crowd' was? This seemingly innocent transition would inevitably change the dynamics of our relationship heavily.

Sam saved some of his precious time for me, but that was usually after he was leaving his new friends. I was now an option to Sam instead of a priority and he let me know that every chance he could get. He would call and show up when he felt like it, but since he was still showing face, he reasoned that he wasn't doing anything wrong.

Now fully accustomed to being at Sam's beck and call, I

began to revolve my plans around when I would be able to spend time with him. I looked pathetic and desperate, but I didn't care: I just wanted to be with him. I convinced myself that once he outgrew this phase in his life, he would care about me again. That didn't happen - it rarely does.

Sam began the new chapter in every teenagers life, when they transition from being an adolescent who doesn't know what it's like to party hard to becoming a teenager who looked forward to partying every weekend. He jumped on the bandwagon and started hanging out with his new respective crowd, even though we all knew he was too deep for the shallowness of high school parties. Even if he didn't want to go, he felt like he had to, so he gave in for the price of being cool.

That year was dark and we both changed. One time, after a night of drinking with his buddies and meeting up with me at our spot afterwards, Sam drunkenly pushes me and I suffer a massive cut on my leg. I walk around for a month with my leg stuck to gauze pads, fighting off an infection. When my mother asks what happened, I lie and tell her I had fallen while playing basketball. It sucked lying to my mother, something I rarely did, but it sucked worse knowing I was protecting somebody who had hurt me.

Another time, Sam was drunk and he spit in my face, much to the anger of our friends who exiled him for a few weeks. I broke up with him but I ended up taking him back, much to my friend's utter dismay. My friends shook their heads at me, while Sasha, Maggie and Molly tried to have a 'Sam Intervention', after spending days consoling me as I cried. They made me meet them at the local pizza parlor and when I got there, I was suddenly aware of everyone expecting something – but I wasn't sure what.

"We're here because we think it's time you stop talking to Sam. He treats you like shit and it's really unfair to us to have to sit there and listen to you cry over this guy when he doesn't give a shit," Maggie said, looking at the girls for support. I rolled my eyes. This was a joke, right?

"We're serious. If you continue on with Sam, we don't want to hear about it anymore. You don't take our advice and we're sick of it," Sasha said.

I took in what they were saying and tried to absorb it, until my beeper went off. I checked and it was Sam, asking to meet up. My friends stared at me, hoping I would make the right decision. I didn't. I promptly got up, putting a quarter in the pay phone and called him back, whispering about our plans for later that night. When I got back, the girls were no longer there and I realized they had left because I had called Sam.

Not even batting an eyelash, I put another quarter in, dialed his number, and waited for him to answer. "My plans fell through, can you pick me up now?" He did, and as we drove past my friends walking on feet, I avoided their stares and looked down. I valued Sam more than my friends at this time…in fact, I valued him more than I valued myself. There was no denying it now.

I had made a choice and it was something I would have to live with when he would introduce me to my first example of betrayal. Seeing as how all of my friendships up until that time had been typical and normal, I was first exposed to how ugly this world could be when he hooked up with one of my best friends behind my back.

*

That year, we all frequently hung out at a place we called "The Pole" - a woodland area in the center of town that housed the American Flag. The girls and I would put Mikes Hard Lemonade in paper cups from the nearby gas station and sip on them as we watched the guys skateboard and the town drive by, going to wherever they had to go. We enjoyed the simplicity of meeting up at the same spot every night and, even though we weren't doing much, we enjoyed our little crew.

Then Tori popped up.

Tori had grown up with Sasha and I, but had moved to a different town so we only saw her on the weekends when she came to Meadows. At the time, Tori had a boyfriend who she had just broken up with, so she came out one night to The Pole with us to get her mind off of things. She immediately set her eyes on Jordan and announced that she was interested in him. I told her I would play matchmaker and ask Sam what Jordan thought of Tori.

Suddenly, she started calling me a lot and asking me to hang out more, always wanting to end up wherever Jordan was. I was her way in and she knew it. Always welcoming, I didn't skip a beat and started spending more time with her regardless of the fact that Jordan made it clear he was not at all interested in her. She kept coming around anyway.

One night, Maggie and I went out with her other friends to an out of town party, while the others routinely went to The Pole for the night. Sam and I weren't exactly on good terms at this point, so I looked forward to a night away from him for once. A few beers later, I fought the urge to drunk-beep him in the hopes that we could maybe meet up before I went home to talk, but I failed miserably. I beeped him from the party-throwers landline with our special code so he knew it was me - but he never called back.

The next day, I had a feeling in my gut something wasn't right, but I couldn't put my finger on what it was. I signed onto AOL and noticed that Sam and Tori both had the same lyrics from an Eagles song on their profile. 'That's weird', I thought to myself, 'She doesn't like classic rock...'

I thought nothing of it until I heard later from Sasha that the night before, Sam had offered Tori a ride home and for some reason, Sam didn't return back to our friends after dropping her off. I knew right away – Sam had hooked up with Tori.

Let me tell you something about instinct: if you have an assumption, follow it. You will 99.9% of the time be right. I didn't want to be right. I wanted to be wrong but unfortunately - I wasn't. I found out that on that car ride the night before, Sam had made a move on Tori and they eventually made out. I was devastated – how could one of my best friends and the guy I loved do that to me? I had been so good to the both of them. I didn't deserve that...and they knew it...they just didn't care. Even worse: I had been the one to introduce them to each other. They had been talking secretly online for weeks and I had no idea.

Needless to say, this revelation shattered my idea of trust. When I asked Tori how could she do that to me, her impassive answer was, "I don't know what I was thinking" and she blamed it on drinking. My inner psychopath came out and I unleashed verbal rampages on them both. I became a person I didn't recognize – angry, bitter, and unreasonable. Nobody was safe – not even myself. I spent weeks moping and became somebody that not even I would want to be around.

I wish I could say that at the time I recognized both of their faults in this tedious betrayal, but as most high school girls believe, I felt as though it was Tori's fault and not his. Once he was over the allure of her, I promptly went back to Sam 'trying to make things work' in the hopes that one day he would once again commit himself to me. Spoiler alert: He didn't.

The friendship I had with Tori never recovered. She went her way and I went mine. We still had mutual friends though and I wasn't at all surprised to hear that a few months later, her life fell apart after she got caught sleeping with her history teacher. Her family basically disowned her and her friends drifted away, appalled by her actions. I felt bad for her but it was karma doing karma's work. She got what she deserved.

No Love

Tori would be the first of a long string of girls that Sam would hook up with in order to hurt me. He developed an even bigger ego knowing he had a girl willing to fight over him but what he didn't know was that he was slowly breaking my heart, piece by piece. It didn't help that one night we went to New York City and, drunk off of Cisco and Mad Dog, he offered to sell me to a pimp in McDonalds in Times Square. I thought he was kidding but he wasn't. I was furious and humiliated so I took the bus ride home alone.

One time at his house, he threw a huge bash and all of our friends were there. After playing some drinking games and drinking mudslides, our friends went home and we slipped off to his room to engage in a drunken heavy make out session. As things started to get wild, he blurted out that he had recently had sex with somebody. I exploded on him - I was still a virgin and had been hoping we would share that moment together. I was devastated because it forced me to look at Sam in a different light, stripping him of perfection. He was no longer one of the good guys – he was now, undisputedly, an asshole. I left his house crying, inconsolable. I never looked at him the same way again.

*

We dragged on this way, with him finding new girlfriends and me plotting to get him back for a long time. I started a few wars with his girlfriends and always ended up broken hearted, crying, and hating everything. Oddly or not so oddly enough, his other girlfriends would too.

I met my match in the form of Rebecca. While I had maintained 'ownership' of Sam for a majority of time, once he met Rebecca, he began to love the attention of two girls in love with him fighting over him, so he caused some fights – actually, a lot of them. He began to see us both at the same time – and we both refused to let the other one "win".

Rebecca was a whole new ballgame when it came to high school drama: she had an evil, mean streak to her. She had the tongue of a serpent and said malicious things that I wouldn't say to my worst enemy – until, of course, she pushed me to that point, which she eventually did. Dealing with Rebecca, I had to grow thick skin and think on the level of a psychopath, and it ended up turning me into somebody I didn't want to be: a bully.

After Sam found out that I had exchanged numbers with a guy at a party, he asked Rebecca to be his girlfriend out of spite. She threw it in my face, purposely making out with him in front of me and boasting about it all over AOL. Knowing Sam better than she did, I took a ride to his house and made sure we made out, just so I could boast about how he cheated on her. She was defeated and he was mine again, but there were no winners in that battle. Just losers.

Thus began a war that I wasn't equipped for, but I tried to bring my best anyway. Regardless of Rebecca and Sam being on and off constantly, it was always me he was running back to. It didn't matter, Rebecca could have very easily kicked my ass and came close a few times – but she found ways to hurt me where it really counted.

One day, my mother asked me if I knew anything about what had happened in the driveway. Confused, I walked outside to see thousands of razor blades on the ground, scattered all the way to my front door. I knew instantly it was Rebecca and her friends because they were the only ones distorted enough to send that kind of message loud and clear - kill yourself - which was something she took much pleasure in telling me to my face every chance she got.

Another time, people were asking me about messages I was sending them on AOL, only I wasn't sending them. I asked a friend of mine for a printout of the conversation and I was stunned to see my screen name accompanying a salacious profile as well as vulgar, filthy messages about my non-existent sex life. I sat in my room studying the messages wondering how they could have possibly signed onto my AOL account and it dawned on me: whoever had done it had made a new screen-name that looked just like mine by changing the i's to lowercase l's.

I ran to my computer and created a new, similar screen-name with different lettering, choosing to capitalize all of the letters. I had a hunch it was Rebecca and her friends, so I instant messaged Rebecca's best friend Courtney (someone that I had never messaged before) to see if she would think it was me or somebody else.

> I SHINE: Hey
> xxxCourtCourtxxx: Rebecca?

My point was proven: why would Courtney think Rebecca was instant messaging her from what appeared to be MY screen-name, if Rebecca hadn't created the fake one?

> I SHINE: No, this isn't Rebecca. I knew she was behind the fake screen-name, thanks so much for confirming it! ☺
> *xxxCourtCourtxxx has logged off.*

I had outsmarted them and they knew it. Rebecca, Courtney, and their equally evil friends conspired to torture me and things only got worse from there. They began to spread vicious rumors about me, telling people I slept around, even though I was still a virgin and had only kissed one person, Sam. Another time, Rebecca grabbed my backpack from my locker and stole my journals, making photocopies of my poetry and throwing them all over the hallway. I cried to Sam and asked him to intervene but he just shrugged his shoulders. I never trusted writing in a journal again.

One day Sasha asked me if I had seen what Rebecca had written on her AOL profile. I hadn't, so I ran to the nearest computer so I could see. I signed onto my account and looked at her profile to see that she had written, in huge, bold letters "BENNY BLACK IS MY HERO."

RAGE.

I went from classroom to classroom looking for Rebecca but I didn't find her because she was sick and hadn't gone to school that day. I did find her that weekend though, while still livid by her elephant-sized balls for writing that on her profile. My friends and I were now at The Pole. A two-door car pulled up, and I noticed Courtney in the passenger side of the car of some guy we went to school with. Knowing wherever Courtney was, Rebecca would be, I started towards the car. Sure enough, she was there sitting in the backseat.

I opened the driver side door, pulled the guy out by his shirt, flipped the seat up and started punching Rebecca directly in her face. Her friends tried to kick me to get me off of her, but the only thing I cared about was breaking this girl in half, so I continued on with tunnel vision. I couldn't let her get away with exploiting my father's death. Rebecca didn't know my father, nor did she know Benny Black, but to take her hatred of me over Sam to that level was surely something she deserved a beating for. So I gave it to her, surprising myself with my own strength.

Apparently, getting your ass kicked in front of tons of people wasn't enough of a reason for Rebecca to keep her mouth shut. I learned this when I was walking into the local deli a few days later to get a bagel for breakfast and Rebecca and her friends were walking in at the same time. While we were inside, they stayed silent, but as they followed behind me as I left, I waited for it.

"Benny Black is my hero," Rebecca cackled, laughing as if this was a new joke and it was hysterical. She had clearly found the button to press if she wanted a reaction from me, and a reaction she got.

I stopped and simultaneously grabbed Rebecca by the hair and threw her against a car, punching her in the face. As her other friends tried to jump me, I turned around and started punching them in the face, getting a few good hits only to return back to Rebecca.

"This...is...it...," I panted, once I was finished. "No more talk about my father. You want Sam, you got him. He's yours." Sam wasn't worth this kind of agony. No guy was. I was calling defeat: I was done.

Dealing with Rebecca was actually a good thing - through dealing with somebody as evil as her, I was forced to toughen up. I could now defend myself because I now had the will to and I didn't need my mommy to fight my battles for me anymore. I chose to use this newfound confidence as a way of intimidating my future enemies. The bullied could become the bully, if necessary. I didn't know whether I should thank Rebecca for bringing this side out of me or resent her.

I became the girl other girls feared bumping into in the school halls, the one you didn't want problems with. The tough girl attitude would be a hard one to break and would be something I would carry along with me well into my mid twenties, when I realized being tough wasn't actually 'cool' – it was just a defense mechanism.

The Promise

I eventually moved on from Sam. It took time, but I did it. He made it easy, once he started hanging out more and more with questionable people, doing questionable things while in college. He began living the kind of life that I didn't want to be around. I found a new boyfriend and Rebecca eventually broke up with Sam for good when she realized that even she deserved better.

After spending too much time being miserable because of the pain Sam had put me through, I was due for a refreshing outlook on love and I found it. When I say I found it, I mean, I really found it.

My junior year, I started dating Dylan. Dylan was funny and endearing, and I found myself attracted to him even though he wasn't the hottest guy in school. He also wasn't the brightest, but he made me laugh for hours and left an impression on me. Dylan asked me to be his girlfriend after a few times of hanging out and I happily said yes.

For the first few months of our relationship, Dylan treated me like a princess. He was the first person to have a real, mutual love for me back. While Sam had played with my emotions after I had told him I loved him, Dylan was the first one to prove he loved me, by showing me instead of just saying it. It was a very sweet love while it lasted: we lost our virginities to each other.

We dedicated ourselves to each other for a good majority of our time. It was a growing experience for me, to actually be in a normal relationship and see that real love was not only possible, but also chaos-free and didn't have to result in razor blades on my driveway.

Sam popped up one night at the diner. I was surprised to see him because he had been away at college and I hadn't heard much from him since. Dylan and I were in the middle of having an argument when Sam, overhearing us, walked up and asked Dylan to go for a walk with him. I was annoyed, wondering what they could possibly have to talk about, but shrugged my shoulders when Dylan looked to me to interject. They went on a walk for about a half hour and came back, Sam shooting a glance my way as he hopped in his friend's car.

"What did you guys talk about?" I asked Dylan, suddenly no longer in the mood to fight over the argument we were having before. Now I was pissed that Sam had intruded in our heated conversation and I had lost momentum.

"Sam was just telling me how I'm a lucky guy to be with you and that while you may be difficult to handle, you're definitely worth it," Dylan answered. "He was cool."

I was surprised because deep down, I was still traumatized by everything that had happened with Sam. The remnants of that relationship would begin to trickle down into my relationship with Dylan. I looked at other girls as enemies and eventually, my constant paranoid jealousy became too much for Dylan and we broke up. He began to date other girls and ended up playing me out with one of them. Once again I was thrown back into another 'crazy' phase – I bullied and threatened the girls who talked to him, clearly not trying to break the cycle I had been a victim of not that long ago.

This time, I was determined to 'win' so unlike with Sam, I fought back against Dylan. I started flirting with guys and found myself engaging in the 'payback' games, most notably hooking up with a former friend of his out of spite. What I didn't realize, was that the only person I was hurting was myself. Call it my own personal version of another really long, drawn out race. I guess I hadn't learned my lesson the first time…

We got back together one last time but eventually, Dylan and I parted ways for good, once we realized that being back together wasn't as much fun as the process of trying to get back together. There were bigger and better things to consume my time with so we went our separate ways but remained friends.

Still, something beautiful happened during that time with Dylan,

I grew the fuck up.

After all of those tense years, Sam and I remarkably became good friends again. Once he graduated college, he moved back home and we kept in touch, even as our lives went into different directions. We hung out occasionally. Sometimes alone, sometimes not, but we always kept it platonic, keeping the past in the past. I would go over his house, we would play NBA Basketball on his PlayStation, and we would have snow day parties at his house with our friends.

Things were different this time around because instead of me chasing Sam, he started to chase me. This time I wasn't willing to be with Sam, which drove him crazy because he hated not having control. He threatened a couple of guys for talking to me until I had to be brutally honest with him that if we were going to be in each other's lives, it was only going to be as friends. He hated it, but since he wanted to be in my life, he accepted it.

One random afternoon, the doorbell rang. I looked at my mother since we didn't get many unexpected visitors, and she rushed to the door. She waved me over, and I was surprised to see Sam standing at the door with an oversized wrapped gift with a big red bow. I opened the screen door and he walked in, putting out his hand to my mom. My mother, always impressed by Sam's gentleman-like demeanor, grabs his hand and shakes it, welcoming him in.

"What's up, Shine?" Sam asks, kissing me on the cheek and handing me the gift.

"What's this?" I ask, sneaking a sly smile.

He winks and then, "Open it."

My mother leaves us alone in the living room as I carefully open my gift as if I am unwrapping a golden Willy Wonka ticket. It is a frame, with an astrological map.

Confused, I look closer and see that on the map is a big, yellow dot. I began to read the pamphlet that is taped to the back of the frame when I realize that Sam had registered a star for me, naming it "Shine". My mouth dropped open.

"What do you think?" he asked, studying my face carefully.

I am lost for words. Never in my life...

He waits for me to say something and suddenly I blurt out, "It's the best gift I've ever gotten in my life." He breaks into a smile. "I love it, I really love it," I say, breathlessly.

My mother peeks her head into the room, smiling at us. "So, what'd you get, honey?"

I show her the frame. "Sam got me a star."

Her mouth drops open, like mine had a few moments earlier. "I didn't even know you could do that."

"I researched it for months and registered with the Star Registry. Your daughter is fascinated with things that shine. Stars, the sun, you name it," Sam explains to my mother, and she politely nods, as if she doesn't know this already by the celestial glow-in-the-dark decals stuck to my bedroom ceiling and the star tattoo that I had unsuccessfully hidden from her.

We both stare at the frame and then back at him. He was pretty extraordinary, more mature and more thoughtful than most guys twice his age. I knew then that I had somebody special in my life. My mother, even more impressed with Sam, winked at us, and left us alone.

"Sam, I really appreciate this gift, but-," I begin, not knowing how to explain that a beautiful gift like that wasn't going to change my feelings towards him.

"Stop," he said, holding up his hands, putting them over his heart, "I just wanted you to have a star of your own. I don't expect anything in return."

It was the sweetest, most heartfelt gesture I have ever been lucky enough to be on the receiving end of. I put the frame on the coffee table and grabbed him, wrapping my arms around his torso, hugging him with all of my might.

*

After I turned 21, Sam would take me out for dinner and drinks, and without fail, we would get drunk and he would claim his undying love for me, apologizing for everything he had done when we were younger. Now that we were both adults, he realized that a 'good one' like me was rare, and he had given me up for juvenile reasons, something he couldn't forgive himself for. I would claim that we were better as friends, which was the truth. I had moved on in more ways than one but I was happy to have still found a true, genuine, loving friend who just so happened to be my first love and an ex.

One night, after consuming lots of drinks and feeling a nice buzz, we sat on top of his car smoking cigarettes underneath the stars, listening to q104.3, like we had done when back when he was seventeen and I was fourteen.

"Where do you think my star is?" I asked him, gazing at the sky. "You know, the one you got me?"

We stared for a few moments and after a couple times of aimless pointing, we both gave up, laughing.

"Shine...promise me something?" he said in all seriousness, staring at the stars, concentrated. I glanced at him and waited for him to continue. "Promise me that you'll put me in your book."

"What book?"

"You're going to write a book one day. I want to be in it."

I looked at him. I figured this was just drunk talk. "K. You'll be in my book," I said, hoping to change the subject.

"Promise?" he asked, urgently.

"I promise," I replied, truly meaning it. I swallowed back a laugh, what would my story be without him in it?

He turned to me and we locked eyes. We were quiet. He looked sad. My heart ached. Even though I had moved on, I still loved him. I always would. It would never work, it hadn't before and it wouldn't now, but still, I loved him.

"Sam?"

"Yeah?"

"How about I dedicate my first book to you? That is, if I actually write one. I mean, who knows?"

Sam grinned his all American smile, the one that I had fallen in love with that night in Ryder's car at Third Street Park and in the food court and all of the millions of times after that. He thought to himself and smirked, "That sounds good. Just don't make me the villain either."

We laughed, absorbing the stars one last time together.

The Union

During most of high school, I surrounded myself with Maggie and Sasha until our senior year, when we started branching out and spending time with other friends. I was surprised to find myself suddenly hanging out with the 'popular' crowd whom I had always thought I was different from. I had depth: I knew loss, I knew pain, I knew strength, and all they cared about was being cool. Still, senior year was about getting to know the people we had grown up with and appreciating our last year together before we all went off into different directions, so I did just that.

At Meadows High, the popular kids weren't assholes like most high school movies portray - except the grade that had teased me for being Ellie Belly, that grade was really in a league of their own. For the most part, the popular guys weren't jerks either; the two hottest guys in my grade just so happened to be the nicest. It was the girls you had to worry about. Promiscuous, bitchy chicks who carried Canal Street knockoff Chanel purses, sleeping with their best friend's boyfriends behind each others backs and judging everyone else when it came time to gossip. These types of girls were common in my high school and I took pride in not being like the rest of them. They were snobs with no redeeming qualities and also not many real friends, because their friendships were based on superficial reasons and not real life.

I won't discriminate, there were some nice popular chicks that were decent enough – those were the ones I associated with. We went to parties together as a group and we pretended to be friends. I got a dose of being one of the cool girls, only to find out it was kind of boring. These girls were too 'vanilla' for me. I wanted to have fun and these chicks were more concerned with being trendy. I eventually started turning them down to hang out to go do my own thing and somehow I fell into the laps of Christina and Blake.

Christina and Blake were the wildest girls in my grade who could out-drink any of the guys we went to school with. Christina and Blake were the complete opposite of the popular girls – they didn't give a shit about fashion, all they cared about was having fun, partying, and dating guys. Suddenly at a crossroads in my teenage life, I realized they were perfect for me so I started hanging out with them.

That year, I entered the partying phase of my high school career. We smoked on weeknights, drank during the weekends and started hanging out with people who had the same interest as us: getting fucked up. Life was now exciting; we stayed out the entire weekend, only going home to shower and sleep before our next adventure. I finally had a dose of excitement in my life.

Christina, Blake, and I were now being invited to the 'secret' parties, quietly thrown by jocks where they could get wasted without the annoying, judgmental chicks watching every thing they did. We were the only girls in attendance because we were getting fucked up with them. Catching wind of this, the popular girls in our grade began to resent us but we didn't care. It wouldn't have mattered if the whole world didn't like us - it was easy to ignore everyone else and seclude ourselves to each other. So we did.

The three of us became attached at the hip senior year and we made it our best year yet. We became a team, us against everybody else. The three of us, reeling from failed relationships, found a kind of understanding and camaraderie that was rare for high school friendships. We became each other's personal therapists and found relief in our endless conversations. It was through our bond that we maintained the kind of friendship that surpassed 'normal' and borderlined dependency. Our friendship was rock solid and nothing could break us apart...or so I thought.

*

Christina, Blake, and I ended up getting accepted into a nearby college. I scored a four-year scholarship, which was a relief to my mother. Maggie went to a university out of state and Sasha went abroad to Italy for international studies. I was sad to see two of my closest friends go off in different directions, but I was grateful to have my two new best friends go to college with me. Excited to start this new chapter in our lives, we basically revolved our school schedules around each other.

Blake and I were seeking degrees in the same field, so we ended up having all of the same classes together. It was good for the both of us because we became competitive with our grades so we were constantly challenging ourselves. During breaks between classes, Blake and I would skip lunch and hit a bowl in our cars in the parking lot, going back to class lit. It was comforting to have someone else share in my horror when I burst into a random case of giggles after a rather long smoke break. The only thing that brought us back to reality was when we noticed the professor staring at us, annoyed. The times we went to class stoned was when I absorbed the most information; I ended up on the Dean's List, much to Blake's annoyance because she didn't.

Christina and Blake were my sorority sisters, without the sorority. We rolled our eyes during Greek Week as sorority girls walked by with marker drawn all over the skin underneath their ridiculous outfits. Christina would mutter under her breath, "All that hazing and those chicks still won't be as tight as us." She was, on some level, right.

We thought we were best friends – but we acted like each other's girlfriends. Three girls with three strong personalities came off as intimidating to the guys we were pursuing; me, with quick sarcastic wit, Christina with her endless need to be right, and Blake's ability to cut you with words. We all also happened to be finding ourselves in broken cycles with losers, which led us to getting too invested in each other's problems. Through hundreds of sob-filled conversations, endless cheering up and tons of broken hearts, Blake, Christina, and I made each other feel whole while simultaneously stunting our chances at other successful relationships.

A friendship between three people is never easy but by our third semester of college, the dynamics of our union became seriously strained when our class times shifted and Christina was getting jealous of the time Blake and I were spending together at school. Our courses ran early in the morning and Christina had to take night courses, which was when we normally hung out during the week. By the time she was getting out of class, we were going home because we had class early the next day. Blake and I spent a significant amount of time without Christina, except on the weekends.

Throw in some competition and hostility, and the resentment got worse. Christina got upset when I knew things about Blake that she didn't, like when Blake and her ex-boyfriend had a crazy fight while Christina had been in class, or when Blake knew more about me than she did. This once-so-strong-yet-now-toxic friendship went on, most times one of us three being on 'the outs' while the other two united together. If Blake was mad at Christina for whatever reason, Blake would be sucking up to me, telling me all the things Christina had said behind my back, and vice versa. This created a never-ending demeaning game of Telephone and always made me wonder, "So this is what my best friends really think about me?"

All of a sudden, major backstabbing began. If I said one thing to one of them, my words were twisted around when being told to the one who wasn't there for the original conversation, leaving me to have to constantly defend myself. They would go to parties without telling me, only for me to have to hear about it when they bragged about it the next day as I sulked. If I had rare plans to meet up with Sasha or Maggie during Spring Break or Christmas Break, Blake and Christina would ignore me for days. After hours of trying to stroke their egos, I would be left with unresolved anger.

One beautiful spring day after a particularly harsh winter, Christina convinced Blake to skip school to hang out with her and Blake didn't bother to tell me. Normally I wouldn't have cared – I wasn't skipping college courses and if Blake did, that was her business – but she had my textbooks in her car that I needed for an open book exam that day. When I got to school, I called Blake wanting to meet up before class.

"Hey, where are you? I need my books," I asked, running up the steps to the cafeteria to get my daily cup of coffee.

"I'm not going today," Blake stated matter-of-factly.

I stopped. "Why not?"

"I don't want to. Christina and I are busy," she answered.

Busy? It was 9:00 in the morning. "Why couldn't you tell me this before I drove all the way to school? There's no way I can make it back before class," I whined.

"Not my problem," she answered, unmoved. I was stunned. She knew exactly what she was doing and I didn't understand why. I angrily hung up, tears flooding my eyes, realizing these 'best friends' of mine kind of sucked.

I was furious and grew only angrier once I got to class to see everyone happily using their textbooks with ease while I had to take my exam, unprepared. I broke out into a sweat and fought back tears as I took an exam that would result in my only D in my college career.

As soon as class was done, I raced to Blake's house. I wanted to know what was so important that the both of them had so boldly disregarded me like I didn't matter. I rang the doorbell to Blake's house and pounded on the door until she answered – I knew her parents were at work.

Blake answered the door and surprised to see me, noticed the look of anger on my face and slammed it shut. I pounded harder, to the point where the walls shook, and it was only then when she opened it slightly. I noticed her glassy eyes. She was lit.

"You screwed me today so that you guys could get high?" I screamed, throwing my shoulder in between the crack to pry the door open fully. Christina was standing nearby, hiding behind the wall. I noticed them give each other knowing looks. They said nothing.

"How could you do that to me? I probably failed my exam," I started, as Blake rolled her eyes. I stared in disbelief. "Are you rolling your eyes at me?"

"Sorry," she said, not meaning it at all.

"What were you thinking?" I asked, hoping for an explanation that would restore my faith in our failing friendship.

"It's nice out today and we wanted to enjoy it," Christina sneered.

"Without me, obviously," I said. Their silence said more than words ever could.

"You realize that I have to maintain a certain GPA to keep my scholarship, right? That exam was 3o% of my grade!" I began to wail, wanting them to feel remorse and to comfort me. They didn't.

"Oh, stop. You're on the Deans List. It's not that big of a deal," Blake said coldly. She didn't understand the significance of being able to go to college for free because my mother couldn't pay the tuition. I needed that scholarship if I was ever going to complete college, obtain a degree, and make something of myself. She wasn't just being heartless, she was jeopardizing my future.

I just stared at them, at a loss for words. These girls didn't care if I was hurt or not, all they cared about was themselves and getting fucked up. This was not friendship. I could no longer base my life on whether or not Blake and Christina were in one of their moods – even though I inevitably would, since we would start a cycle of a fluctuating on/off friendship that would span with years in between.

*

Being stuck in a pattern of on/off with Christina and Blake, I missed my friends who were now off at college, living new and exciting lives, while I was stuck local, doing the same shit I had been doing since high school. Maggie had fallen in

120

love with a guy she met at school and moved in with him, starting a domestic life way before any of the rest of us. We didn't have much in common anymore so we lost touch and sadly, only saw each other around the holidays.

Thankfully, I still had Sasha. I found myself confiding in her while she was abroad, racking up huge phone bills. We spent every night on the phone, filling each other in on what the other was missing, even though she wasn't missing much. I counted down the days until Sasha came home and when she did, I was waiting on her doorsteps, ready to greet her like a childhood pet. Sasha had been consistent throughout my life and I considered her my one true best friend, aching for her when she was away.

Living in Italy had enthralled Sasha and she came home a very different person than the girl I had grown up with: she was an even bigger diva than before. Each time, it was harder to tolerate. Since she had moved and seen a different side of the world, she reasoned that she had more life experience than everyone else, and thus, she thought of herself as more accomplished. I expected Sasha to be excited to see me, only to find myself with a bored Sasha that did nothing but brag about her exciting life back in Italy.

I was jealous. Here I was, doing nothing with myself other than working, going to classes, and spending a majority of my time with frenemies, while Sasha was living the good life.

Though she sympathized with my troubles with Christina and Blake, Sasha didn't really care. She was home only for short periods of time and her real life was in Italy, outside of Meadows, where she had a new best friend...and a better life outside of Jersey. She was cutting ties with her young life to embrace her adult life. I couldn't blame her...but I still winced every time she flipped her hair and looked at me with pity before saying, "I'd like, die, if I was stuck in Meadows like you. That must suck."

Sasha would realize just how much it did suck, when her father, who had been paying her tuition, had to file for bankruptcy that summer before she went back to school. As a result, her father ordered her to stay home and go to a local college to finish her degree because it was more affordable than the international university she had been going to. She was devastated, not being able to go back to her grandiose life, and beside herself knowing she had to stay home in boring ole' Meadows.

As soon as she got the news, I slept over her house for a week and consoled her as she wailed about being back to 'reality'. She cried for days, all through the night, and it eventually irked me to see her put herself through such hysterics over moving back home. She was acting like we lived in the slums of the world. I grew impatient, because as much as I craved a change of scenery myself, Meadows wasn't that bad.

After a few weeks of dealing with Sasha sulking around and being bitchy, I called her out on her dramatics. "You need to relax."

She narrowed her eyes at me. "Am I supposed to be happy, being back in Meadows?"

"You're acting like Meadows is the worst place in the

world," I said, defending our hometown that I was just as much over as Sasha was.

"It is!" Sasha screamed, startling me.

"No it isn't!" I screamed back. There, I admitted it.

"How would you know? You've never been anywhere but Meadows. You'll probably die here, like the rest of the townies!" she screamed, her words stinging me like electric currents. Fighting back tears, I left her house, slamming the door, wondering if she was right.

I found myself, once again, questioning my friendship with another person I had known as a best friend. Sasha apologized the next day but the damage was done. She had confirmed the one thought I had fought all of those years: she looked down on me. How could our friendship go back to the way it was, now that I knew that she felt that way?

I tried to be a good friend to her as she suffered the rest of that year adjusting to being back home. She adapted, and I chalked the incident up to 'Sasha having a Sasha moment', going on as if that conversation never happened. I just had to hope for the best. Clearly I was a better friend to her then she was to me and knowing that it was the same deal with Christina and Blake, I realized that the saddest aspect of my life was that I would never find a friend like myself.

*

This was all I needed to start distancing myself from the girls, which gave me a lot of open time to immerse myself in new friendships. I started hanging out with friends from school and people I worked with. It was liberating, being free like that, and I lived, taking on new jobs and new relationships on my own, without anyone breathing down my neck. It was hard at first, but it was time to start deciding - and living - for myself. For so long, I had depended on my best friends for approval of many things, and it was time to start validating things myself. There was so much more out there besides the confinement of these chicks and it was time to go see... alone, if necessary.

I would continue to spend some significant time with Sasha, Christina, and Blake. Still, I couldn't deny that these once-solid friendships were actually pretty fragile and not as strong as I had thought. I was in need of something unbreakable, the kind of friendship that embraces the good times and endures the hard times. It would be during this period that I found my future best friends, enlightening me that sometimes, your lifelong ride-or-die's end up being the ones you least expect.

Notorious Thugs

Vince Hartman and I had gone to elementary school together, but we had never been close. During our childhood he was considered a "genius" because he had an impressively high intelligence and he was on the honor roll every single quarter. Once we hit middle school, Vince decided that he wanted to be a 'bad boy' so he became one, and as a result he spent his high school years going where bad boys go: a place for 'troubled kids'. He left behind a group of guys, his best friends, who were considered the rebels of my grade. These guys listened to violent rap music, drank and smoked before anybody else did, and they had a habit of skipping school. They truly didn't give a damn – and that's what made them so much cooler than everybody else.

During one of the rare times that Christina, Blake and I are actually getting along effortlessly, we drive past Vince and almost break our necks when we catch sight of him. We hadn't seen Vince in about four years, but those years had done him good. Vince was now jacked, his shoulders ripping through his shirt, and he had his hair tied up in boxed braids. He was carrying a case of beer and walking towards his new apartment down the block. As Blake slowed down, he looked in the car window and caught us staring at him. He looked away.

"Damn, Vince got HOT," Christina said, as Blake quickly drove away, still staring out the back window at Vince's ass. She was almost drooling.

"I wonder what he's up to now," I said. The girls shrugged.

The next day, I found out. Blake was having us over her house so I stopped by the liquor store to pick up some wine, only to be standing next to Vince in line at the check out. He looked over at me and smiled a genuine smile.

"How the hell are you?" Vince asked.

"I'm good," I answered somewhat awkwardly, thinking of the day before when he caught us checking him out like creeps. Also, I wasn't good with small talk. The silence lingered as we waited to be checked out.

"What are you getting into tonight?" Vince asked, breaking the silence, propping his case of beer on the counter.

"Same shit, having some drinks and getting lit," I replied. He raised his eyebrows, shocked that I was talking about smoking. I had seemed like such a goodie-goodie growing up and he hadn't been around when I had turned slightly rebellious.

"Oh yeah?" he laughed, amused. The clerk began to ring

126

up his things.

"Yeah," I said defensively. I was 'hip' now and he needed to know that.

"Let me get your number so we can get together soon," he said, grabbing his bags.

I paused. I didn't see that coming. He was struggling with his bags so I grabbed a nearby napkin and using the pen provided for lottery tickets, I scribbled my number on it and put it in his pocket. He said goodbye, and I bought my things and went to Blake's.

"I just ran into Vince Hartman at the liquor store," I mentioned casually as I poured a glass of wine.

"Oh yeah? Did he look as sexy as he did yesterday?" Christina asked.

I hadn't noticed. "I wasn't paying attention. He asked me for my number though."

That stopped Blake and Christina in their tracks. They put their glasses of wine down and stared at me. "He asked you for your number?" Christina asked.

"Yeah," I said, sipping my wine.

Blake widened her eyes and made a face.

"Why?" Christina asked, jealousy in her voice.

"Why what?"

"Are you going to hang out with him?"

"He was making small talk. You know how awkward I get. He was probably just being polite."

Silence.

I knew what they were thinking – because I was thinking it too. In a town where we grew up basing social status on prior high school opinions, Vince and his crew were cooler than everyone else because they were untouchable. They didn't allow outsiders in unless they were worthy. Christina and Blake didn't think I was cool enough to hang out with that group of guys – and deep down, I thought they were right – but they also didn't want me spending my free time with anyone but them. I wasn't surprised when they froze me out of their conversation for the entire night, as I sat back quiet, annoyed, and feeling alienated.

I was surprised the next day when Vince actually called me, inviting me to a party that he was having at his place that night. A bunch of guys I grew up with were going, and I figured that at least if I was in unknown territory, I would have people there that I knew. It helped that Christina and Blake were giving me the silent treatment over the discovery that I may actually want to spend time with people besides them. I mean, how many times could we spend our nights smoking, drinking, and complaining about our exes? So I went. Alone.

I didn't need backup. Regardless of the fact that I was the only girl at Vince's that night, I had a great time hanging out with his crew. We drank, we caught up, and I held my own, even if a few skeptics were side-eying me for the first few hours. I appreciated the good vibes in the room that had been seriously lacking everywhere else I went.

Vince called me the next day and asked me to lunch. I said sure, and he picked me up and we went to get sandwiches. What should have been a twenty minute lunch session turned into a six hour conversation about everything that we had both been through the last few years that he had been MIA. He filled me in on life away from Meadows and his truly wild teenage years. I was humbled to learn that Vince was so much more than a good-looking 'bad boy' – he was a young man who wanted a normal, boring life, the kind I was yearning to escape from.

It was mind-blowing, hearing his heartfelt stories, and I was surprised that Vince chose to confide in me, a chick from Meadows who he hadn't seen in years. He was open and honest, yet realistic: he knew his choices had gotten him to where he was. I saw a sense of bold determination in him to not fall back into bad patterns. He was better than his reputation, and he knew it. This time, he was wiser because now, he was grown.

From that point on, Vince and I became very close. I had been seeking out a solid friend and he had been seeking out a confidant, and we found both in each other that summer. We went to concerts together, we went out for drinks together, and we spent most nights at his apartment hanging out. In time, I became best friends with not only him, but with most of The Guys. I eventually became a part of their group. It was crazy – but it happened.

The best part about being a girl in a group among guys was that I no longer had to feel that pit in my stomach every time I met up with the girls who fully stopped their conversation as if I had invaded some secret that I wasn't allowed to be included in. If you walk into a room and everyone stops talking, they were probably talking about you. I knew this from experience and I appreciated that I didn't have to deal with that with The Guys. The Guys didn't talk shit because The Guys kept it real.

Like, really real. "Stop crying over him, he doesn't care about you either way, so get over it." "That dress is way too short, don't complain when you're getting hit on by creeps all night." "You shouldn't drink Red Bull & vodka." The Guys pulled no punches and were brutal with non-sugarcoated honesty. They provided something that I had been in desperate need of for a long time: trust.

Vince and The Guys became an imperative support system in my life. When Christina, Blake and I would get into a melodramatic argument and I would call Vince crying, he would tell me that "three's a crowd" and that it was time to let go of people who wanted my company just to commiserate. He was right: my friendship with the girls had reached unhealthy proportions. Soon enough, I was with The Guys every single day, only hanging out with the girls once in a blue moon.

Here's the crazy part about my relationship with The Guys: there was no sex involved. We were really just friends. Outsiders thought I was secretly hooking up with one of The Guys behind everyone's back, but I really wasn't. Although there were a few drunken nights when lines could have been crossed, they weren't. The Guys were important to me and I enjoyed spending time with them platonically, for no other reason than being happy when I did.

Luckily for me, I happened to be the kind of friend that The Guy's girlfriends actually liked – I was harmless, and around these people because I loved them, not because I 'liked' them. As a result, I became a confidant for most of their girlfriends too. I've been so involved in Vince's love life that I joke about charging him for relationship therapy sessions. I wouldn't have it any other way though – The Guys can trust me and I can trust them – and I consider it an honor being the one they look to as a 'female voice'. They know all of my secrets and they've kept my skeletons to themselves – something females couldn't do even if you promised money for their silence.

I finally found the kind of loyal, united, and loving friends I had been waiting for all of my life, who just so happened to be people I had known all of my life. The Guys became my brothers in every sense of the word. I felt like I was the youngest sister in a family of all older boys: they had my back to such a degree that I felt safe around them. I developed a feeling of security that nobody could touch. Sure I could handle myself, but it gave me confidence knowing The Guys wouldn't let me because now, I was a part of their family.

The Guys remain some of my favorite people on Earth, and to this day, Vince is still my best friend.

*

With all of the guy friends I had, I was bound to meet other guys through them and from this I learned a valuable lesson that you can't understand unless it happens to you: don't hook up with anyone whose friendship you value. What they say is true...if you hook up with a good friend, it could ruin your friendship and things will never be the same.

A friend I had met through The Guys, Dean, started bombarding me with requests to hang out. Dean was the oddball within The Guys - while most of The Guys dressed in Ecko and Rocawear, Dean's idea of casual attire were Armani dress shirts and black dress pants. He took pride in his appearance and as a result, he came off as classy and put together. We were spending more and more time together at Vince's and we eventually ended up hanging out on our own. Dean was fun to be around and we enjoyed taking long car rides, listening to indie music. We eventually became very good friends.

Dean was so handsome that he was regularly mistaken for a model. He came from a good family and he was a gentleman in every sense of the word. Dean started asking me to hang out more and more and eventually, we were together everyday. Seeing as how I was a girl he could talk to and he enjoyed spending time with me, he started hinting at having feelings for me.

I didn't bite at first. At this point, I was just enjoying hanging out with The Guys and wasn't really looking for a relationship, so I turned down his attempts at turning our friendship into something more. The only men I wanted in my life were as friends because I was enjoying being single and not having to worry about anybody but myself.

Dean persisted. One night he caught me off guard by grabbing my face to kiss me and after realizing that he was actually a good kisser, I gave in, surprising myself as I kissed him back. The day after we kissed, we went to a party at Vince's together as two people officially 'talking'. It was a weird night and our being together wasn't well received by The Guys. They didn't want 'internal dating' within the group because they foresaw it ending in a disaster. Some of our friends thought I would rip Dean's heart out, but those who knew better knew he would rip out mine.

He suggested that we go up to his parent's house in the Poconos that weekend. We would go Friday night and spend some time alone, and our friends would meet us down there Saturday afternoon. I agreed, looking forward to a weekend in the mountains and curious to see where this 'thing' would go.

I felt pressured to measure up to what I thought his attractive look deserved: an equally attractive girl. So I put on more makeup than usual and I wore my best Juicy Couture velour sweater with my Rock and Republic jeans. When he picked me up, he had a sly smile on his face and he commented, "You don't need all that makeup. You're pretty without it." I nuzzled up to his face and smiled. He was a smooth-talker and he was suddenly so sexy. At first I didn't think him and I made sense, but now I couldn't imagine being with anybody else. As he drove, we held hands. It should have been awkward, but it wasn't. It was smooth and easy, almost as if we were acting on the inevitable. It felt right.

We arrived at his house that was nestled right on a lake, outfitted in sprawling grounds. His boat bobbed against the deck and I marveled in the beauty of this home that was sadly left alone during parts of the year. He showed me around and as soon as we got settled, Dean made some fancy martinis and we relaxed on his front porch, enjoying the fresh air.

Once it was time for dinner, he went into the kitchen and started cooking, leaving me to take in the picturesque scenery in solitude. He packed a picnic basket and led me to the lake, where we ate dinner while enjoying the water flow past us freely. It was charming. That night we laughed a lot. It was a sweet feeling, being wanted by a guy who liked me for the right reasons, and I felt as though I was breaking out of my life-long habit of caring about guys that didn't give a shit about me.

When we went back to the house after eating, I had butterflies in my stomach because I knew in a matter of moments, we would be heading to his bedroom. It was time to be real about 'this thing', and there were no more chances for me to back my way out. Except this time, I didn't want to. I wanted to sleep with him. I wanted to kiss him and have him kiss me and feel the intimacy from someone that I knew had feelings that were genuine and real.

Once we were in his bedroom, we enjoyed the moonlight seeping through the window, and fell into each other as we began to make out. It was our time to set upon what had been in the makings for quite a while and I thought the sex would be glorious.

Except, it wasn't.

The whole act ended quicker than it took to start up and I unintentionally made a "That's it?" kind of face to myself. Dean noticed and was so embarrassed that he recoiled from me. As soon as we looked at each other, it was instant awkwardness. We recovered ourselves and set out to go downstairs to go to sleep in complete silence. I whispered to him that it wasn't a big deal, but he crossed his arms and ignored me for the rest of the night.

The next day, our friends arrived. We swam in the lake,

rode UTV's and played games, all the while he and I didn't even look at each other. He barely spoke a word to me and spent most of his time closed off. He was nasty and copped an attitude with our friends. It became a situation I didn't want to be around, but he had driven me and I had no ride home, so I had to deal.

As hours went on and the situation became more uncomfortable, I was starting to lose my patience. Being embarrassed was one thing, but treating me like I had done something wrong was another. I tried to stop him in the hall and talk to him, but he walked past me and ignored me. This enraged me and we got into a huge screaming match that went on for hours in front of everybody, to the point where Vince had to step in and defend me. I couldn't believe somebody I thought I knew so well had turned into a monster as soon as I had given into him. In order to keep the peace, I was basically thrown into the basement, left to my own devices, to sleep alone.

He refused to drive me home and since it was clear I was no longer welcome there, Vince had to cut his weekend short to drive me back, fighting the urge to say, "I told you this would happen." The whole car ride, all I could do was zone out, look out the window and think about how bummed I was.

I wondered to myself if it was just me, or if this was typical. Did sex really matter that much? Didn't the connection between two people matter more? Was I naïve not to know these things at my age?

Either way, I had learned my lesson: never, ever hook up with somebody you have a genuine friendship with, hot or not. Most of the time it doesn't work out and if it doesn't, you could lose an important friend forever.

We never spoke again.

Turn The Page

Still in college, I got hired as a waitress at a restaurant. The owners were a married couple from the south and they had no idea how to handle a business on the east coast. The fact that they valued drugs more than profits didn't help either, but I quickly learned not to bat an eyelash when they were running upstairs to indulge while the bartender and I ran the floor. I did what I had to do, taking on responsibilities that I wasn't being paid for, but I enjoyed the job and the atmosphere so I didn't mind. I got close to a few of the people I worked with as well as some regulars, including Neil, a friendly family man who offered to buy me a car when my car broke down. I politely declined but I appreciated his offer, happy just knowing there were people like him around.

The bartender, Scarlett, was a pretty punk chick with blue hair, piercings in weird places and faint crimson scars on her arm from years of self-abuse. During one of our first conversations she had bragged about beating an addiction to opiates at some point in her teenage years as well as surviving being sexually abused as a child. We eventually got to know each other during dead shifts where we would take shots and chat.

Scarlett's boyfriend was in a rock band that was on tour so she spent a majority of time home with her cats drinking by herself. She didn't have many friends (she had moved to New Jersey to be with her boyfriend after living most of her life in Philadelphia) and complained of feeling lonely. She had started bartending as a way to meet new people and hopefully make new friends.

One Saturday afternoon after we were done with our lunch shifts, Scarlett asked me to come over to her apartment and hang out. I looked at the clock. I had plans around 8pm with The Guys but that was hours away so I figured, what the hell. I could kill two birds with one stone by keeping her company while wasting time before I had to go out.

The apartment she lived in with her boyfriend was cute and very inviting, decorated with tons of plants and lit candles. The vibe was romantic, with the walls painted in pink hues lit up by dim lights. As she gave me a tour of her place, I couldn't help but notice copious amounts of pill bottles in the kitchen, on her nightstand, and on a shelf in the living room. Considering her upbringing, I minded my business and ignored it.

She poured us two glasses of wine and we started talking. She got pretty buzzed within an hour, but because I had to eventually drive back to Meadows, I only took a few sips. There was an episode of *The Hills* on and as I went to reach for the remote to change the volume, she grabbed my arm. I looked at her.

"What do you think of me, Ellie?" she asked.

"I'm so thankful to have you at work!" I said, meaning it. She was the only other person at the restaurant my age and we had become friendly pretty quickly.

"Is that it?" she pressed.

"What do you mean? I think you're cool, or I wouldn't be sitting in your living room with you on a Saturday afternoon."

She smiled a mischievous smile. "Do you like me?"

Huh? I was confused. "Of course. Why else would I be here if I didn't like you?" It's not like I made a habit of spending my rare free time with people I didn't like. I could barely find time for the people I did like.

She rolled her eyes, as if she was getting frustrated. "Have you ever kissed a girl before?"

"No," I answered. Why was she asking me these questions?

"Do you want to?" she asked, edging closer to me on the couch. Her face was suddenly way too close to mine.

"I'm not into girls," I said slowly, inching away from her. She came closer and put her hand on my leg.

This was getting awkward quick.

"Come on...you're so pretty...I've been wanting to kiss you since I met you. Don't you feel that spark?" she asked, rubbing my leg.

I didn't. Not even a little bit. I shook my head, removed her hand, and pointed to the pictures of her boyfriend on the walls. "What about your boyfriend?"

She laughed wickedly, threw her hair over her shoulder, and for the first time I saw a bit of evil in her dark eyes. I shuddered. "Oh please, he's on tour probably fucking random groupies all over the country." She tried to look nonchalant, but I could tell that the fact that this could have been true weighed on her. Still, I wasn't going to make out with her just so she could settle some invisible score with her absent boyfriend.

I tried to change the subject, carefully. No success.

"Why don't you like me? I'm not pretty enough for you? You think you'll find somebody out there better than me?" she accused, icily. She was coming on way too strong.

"Yes and that person will have a dick," I answered. It was harsh but it was the truth. She fell back into the couch, crossing her arms, and stared at the TV.

It was time to go. "I have to go home and get ready for my plans tonight. I'll see you Monday at work." She ignored me and didn't answer back. I closed the door behind me and shook off a feeling of uneasiness.

I didn't see her Monday. She switched her shift with another bartender and I would be lying if I said that I wasn't relieved. I worked that day but had exams that entire week so I took off a majority of my shifts to focus on writing papers and studying.

The next Monday, exams were over and I was excited to go into work, make some money and be around people that had nothing to do with the English department at my college. I parked my car, opened the door, and was surprised to see the

140

owners and the rest of the staff in the middle of a heated discussion.

I slunk to the side quietly, not wanting to interrupt. "What's going on?" I whispered to the chef.

"Scarlett and Julio got drunk here last night during their shift. They must have left together and this morning Julio woke up to police officers, arresting him for rape. They are waiting for the results of the rape kit they did on her. He swears she made it up. He is devastated."

I couldn't believe it. Julio was the Executive Chef, a handsome man who had a better work ethic than anybody I had ever met. He was a gentleman, always treating everyone around him with respect, and he was more than grateful for the opportunity to work. His wife had suffered from an illness since she had given birth to their second child, and Julio broke his ass to make ends meet. All he ever did was talk about his family.

I had seen many women hit on Julio during my time at the restaurant, to no avail. He was committed to remaining loyal to his wife. When I once remarked about a customer calling him sexy, Julio stated that he was at the restaurant to make money, not to 'play games'. "This," he motioned towards his messy chef's station, "is all for my family." I was impressed and secretly hoped that I would find a man to love me as much as Julio loved his wife.

For that reason, the story didn't make sense. Sure, Julio drank afterhours when the restaurant was closed, but we all did. How drunk could he have gotten? I thought to two Saturday's ago when Scarlett had made a move on me and how cold she had been when I turned her down. It was like there were two Scarlett's: the person at work and the person outside of work. Which one left with Julio?

The already-fragile restaurant was now undeniably torn. Scarlett quit. Julio remained in jail because his wife wasn't able to afford bail, so the cooks pooled their checks together to get him out. The owners were pissed that Julio and Scarlett had brought unwanted attention to the restaurant, the cooks were convinced Scarlett had manipulated whatever had happened between the two of them, and the bartenders and waitresses were convinced that Scarlett had been raped. I remained silent, convinced that Julio was telling the truth.

Business went on as usual. A few months later, one of the restaurant's regulars came in to tell us a shocking story about Scarlett. She had found a new bartending job in another town nearby and had hooked up with one of her customers, eventually inviting him back to her place. He woke up the next morning disorientated on his whereabouts and didn't understand why there were cops looking over him, ready to arrest him for sexually assaulting Scarlett the night before.

This time, Scarlett had been sloppy and she forgot to hide the pills on the shelf in the living room. One of the bottles just so happened to be Flunitrazepam, commonly known as roofies or the date rape drug. As the cops were about to put handcuffs on this guy who was now sobbing on the sofa while Scarlett was in the doorway, arms crossed and unaffected, one of them noticed the pill bottles out of the corner of his eye.

After investigating, the cops realized that this girl had

pressed charges on Julio for rape a few months earlier. After some intense questioning, the truth came out, she had roofied the guy the night before. Back at the police station, after being charged with drugging her customer, they focused on the case with Julio.

Noticing holes in her previous story, they pressed even harder and she eventually admitted to drugging Julio that night at the bar and bringing him back to her house to have sex. She tried to seduce him but he couldn't get hard and while he was passed out, she tried to have sex with him anyway.

When the police asked Scarlett for an explanation on why she would do these things, her answer was as pathetic as it was infuriating, "I wanted my boyfriend to come home." She admitted that she thought if she had called him while he was on tour, told him that she had been raped, he would come back home to save her and basically know better than to ever leave her again. He did eventually come home, but only to pack up his things and move to Florida to live with some girl he had met at one of his concerts.

The last thing I heard of Scarlett was that she had joined a traveling circus as a ticket seller, her only option to pay off civil lawsuits and legal fines. Julio found a new job and the staff at the restaurant threw him a goodbye party. I asked him how he was feeling now that the entire 'situation' was over.

He grinned a thankful smile and answered, "No hay mejor sensación que cuando se descubra la verdad."

"What does that mean?" I asked.

"There is no better feeling then when the truth sets you free."

Glory Days

After the Scarlett saga, I was eventually asked to bartend and I enjoyed making drinks so much that I knew I would never go back to waitressing. There is a totem pole in the service industry and once you bartend, it's hard to go back. Unfortunately, months later the owners lost control of the restaurant and the new chef and myself ended up running the entire restaurant on our own. We managed for a while, but we didn't know how to run a business, and neither did the owners. The restaurant eventually closed down and I was left without a job so I immediately started looking into other places.

A good friend of mine suggested I get a job bartending at Harley's, a family-run bar in town that had been one of my father's favorite local watering holes. I immediately refused, considering myself 'better than that', working at a place where, what I considered to be drunks, hung out. I compared every local bar in town to a place where alcoholics went, simply because that's where my father had spent his last few years alive: at town bars, instead of with me.

For a long time, I associated men drinking alcohol to 'townies', better known as 'local lifers'. In fact, anybody that hung out at town bars were. This ignorance would take a long time to grow out of - but I ultimately felt that if you had to have a beer before you went home to your family, there was something selfish about that. 'Stop drinking, go home, and be with your family,' I imagined my father, given the chance, would tell these people if he were able to.

I'll never forget the time one of the local drunks randomly rang my doorbell at 3:30 am, looking for a place to pee. When my mother told him to get lost, he pleaded, "I knew your husband, just let me piss." My mother refused, telling him he was scaring me, and slammed the door in his face. I had nightmares for weeks. This experience only solidified my opinion that alcoholics were scary.

A close friend of mine, Tyler, was best friends with Katie, the manager of Harley's, and she just so happened to be looking for someone to cover the shifts of a bartender who had just moved. I voiced my concerns about working at a 'townie bar' to Tyler and he insisted I try it and 'get over' myself. He was right, I was being a snob, so I said I would check it out.

We went into Harley's that night for a drink so Katie and I could get to know each other and she could show me around. The smell of cigar smoke, old school Italian cologne, and whiskey filled the air and I found myself getting nostalgic chills as I walked behind the bar. I already knew Katie, she was a senior when I was in middle school, and I had always heard how nice she was – but I was surprised to see how friendly she actually was in person. Katie had a permanent smile on her face and the fact that she was always in a good mood, knew how to have a good time, and genuinely cared about people made her a hit in our small town. She was the kind of person to spot out the creep in a bar and warn the girl sitting by herself, protecting her when the guy would inevitably stroll over and attempt to hit on her.

The fact that Katie was already in her thirties and had surpassed all of that bullshit girl drama made her the perfect fit for me. I desperately needed a female friend who had already gone through everything I was going through to tell me, "Once you hit your thirties, you're not going to give a shit about any of the things you stressed out about during your twenties." She was, of course, right.

Katie hired me. My first few shifts I kept to myself, making drinks and serving them, only to retreat back to my corner to be alone to stare at my phone. I was intimidated by this crowd; bikers, misfits, and townies. I came off as thinking I was better than everybody there and was ashamed to be working at a place where my father had hung out, at a place I had looked down on my whole childhood. I didn't tell my friends I was bartending there at first because I was so embarrassed. It would take a few months to outgrow that ignorance, but over time I would learn that these barflies were more than customers, they would become friends. Some would even become family.

*

Budweiser Bob was a customer that had been coming into the bar long before I worked there. An Italian-looker-by-the-book, he would come in after working exhausting hours for a beer before he went home. He never got drunk though, he just liked the taste of beer. I liked and respected that about him.

The time he came in was usually our busiest so we never had a chance to talk at first. During that year in college, most of my classes were late at night so I took on a lot of day shifts at the bar. At that time of the day, the bar was usually very quiet so I spent a lot of my time doing homework on my laptop, waiting for people to come in but not really caring if they did or didn't.

Bob came in one afternoon for a beer before he had to get to another night of grueling work as a contractor working in south Jersey. As he walked in, I shut off my laptop and set myself in front him. "What will it be today, Bob? Let me guess, a Bud?" He nodded, amused that I still bothered to ask. All he ever drank was Budweiser.

Since there was nobody else there, we started talking. He was born in Long Island and I had always thought that he was secretly in the mob because he looked like a quintessential Mafioso guy, so I asked him if he was. He scoffed, "Waddya kiddin' me with that?" I laughed, knowing that anybody that passed him on the street probably thought the same thing but still, he didn't hold it against me.

What I liked most about Bob was that he wasn't a creep.

148

Working in a bar, any bar, as a single 22-year-old chick is like throwing yourself to the wolves. I've been hit on by fathers of the people I grew up with, politicians, and high profile married men. I learned pretty quickly that some men were pigs, so I made my stance clear by becoming the 'bitchy bartender' that was impossible to get. Somehow, that made those types of men want me even more.

Bob wasn't about that. In fact, he set the precedent for men respecting me when they were at the bar in his presence. He had three daughters and looked at me like I was someone's kid instead of a piece of meat, and he treated me with the utmost respect. I appreciated it.

In a bar full of people, when Bob came in, everybody knew I was going to be attached to him for the rest of the night indulging in many of our hundreds of in-depth conversations. My friends would scoot over to where he was sitting because they knew that was where I was planted until he left to go home, but also to catch some of his never-ending wisdom in earshot.

I was questioning God and spirituality a lot during this time and being someone who I looked up to, I asked Bob about his thoughts on God one night. "YOU'RE God," he said pointing his finger to my head. "The universe, religion, it's all in you." He explained that there was no specific God, because every human was their own God. Each person was the master of his or her own destiny. The universe was your mind and Heaven was life on Earth.

"The reason you are struggling is because you keep asking questions to a person who can't answer them for you.

Instead of seeking answers from God, you gotta start asking yourself some questions. Explore yourself and you'll get your answers. Then do something about it." I had never looked at things that way before and maybe it was time to. Valuing his words, I started looking inward instead of outwards.

Some highlights of our many conversations stem from the times he came in and our roles reversed because I needed him to be an ear to hear me out. One of the most resounding pieces of advice he gave me was in regards to my girl friends who were leaving a bitter taste in my mouth: "The lay of the land is very important. Always be aware of your surroundings, and most importantly, the people around you. You walk into a place and you think everyone is your friend, those are the ones who get you." He knew what he was talking about, as I would unfortunately come to find out later.

I learned more from Bob then he could ever learn from me. He wasn't a customer, he was a genuine friend. Within time, he became like a father figure to me - which was good, because working at Harley's became an instant reminder that mine wasn't around.

*

Bartending as an adult at a place where my father hung out as an adult himself was enlightening because I was able to hear stories from people who had spent their own glory days with him. Still, I had to relive my father's death, an event I hadn't even been old enough to comprehend at the time, as soon as Meadows old-timers came in and asked me what my

150

last name was. A routine conversation that happened more often than not:

"So, are you from around here?"

"Yep."

"You're from Meadows?"

"Yes, born and raised."

"What's your name?"

"Elodie, but most people call me Ellie."

"What's your last name?"

I tell them.

Slight pause. "Are you related to the one that was killed at that bar down the street?"

"Yeah, that was my father."

Awkward silence. If the guys knew my father well enough or had grown up with him, there would be tears in their eyes which always, for some reason, annoyed me. One guy even had to go outside one time to 'collect himself' because he got so emotional. Either way, once somebody found out who I was, there was always an uncomfortable silence that penetrated the air.

Then, "I knew Benny Black. He was a sick mother-fucker."

I never knew how to reply to that other than to say, "Oh yeah?"

"Yeah, my buddy beat Black up at a bar one time. He ripped a pay phone out of the wall and bashed him with it."

I say nothing.

"Sick guy. I mean, why else would he stab his wife to death?"

"Yeah," I reply in a daze, before scattering away and avoiding them the rest of my shift.

Another time, a police officer was hanging out at the bar with a friend of his before going to a concert. We were in the middle of a conversation when I noticed his friend looking at me as if he should know me from somewhere. The friend asked me my last name. I sighed before telling him.

"I know that last name," he says before turning to the cop and saying, "Hey remember when that nutcase Benny Black beat up that guy at that bar?"

The cop nods before saying, "Yeah, I was on the scene. It wasn't pretty." He thinks to himself for a moment and shakes his head, "His victim was a really nice guy."

"Do you have any relation to him?" the friend asks, looking at me as he sips his beer.

Katie, overhearing this, interrupts and warns, "That's his daughter."

Their mouths drop and they stare for a moment. "You're his daughter?" I nod.

"I knew your father very well. We lived down the street from each other and we used to play sports together. He was a great man," the cop says gently.

"Cool," I say, dazing out again.

"Man, that was really an awful time in Meadows," the friend says. "Two local guys, and the good guy got killed by the bad guy. Tough times."

I stare at him and silently wish for magical powers to make him disappear on the spot. The magical powers don't come through and I am forced to endure more nostalgic talk about my father.

Most people in my position would probably get sick of these occurrences but after the rawness of having that wound reopened subsided, I got used to it and found it satisfying to make it clear that not only was I my father's daughter, but that I was doing well for myself. I was proud telling these men that I was a writer in college and would be graduating with two degrees. I knew that most people would assume, with the life I had been given, I would be doing very differently.

I felt vindicated when these strangers, who knew me as a child and were now meeting me again as an adult, sat back in their chair, arms crossed, grinning as they said, "Well, good for you." "I'm sure your father is very proud." "I'm so happy to know you are doing well." "Your mother raised you well." I felt as though even though the beginning of my story had been written way before I could tell it, now I had control, and I had the power to write my own chapters. I was able to impact my own story, regardless of the past, and if I was smart, I'd change it for the better. This was my time.

*

I believe that Harley's is haunted - not in a spooky way – but in a good way. I am shown signs all the time, like the cash register popping open when certain songs come on, the doors locking on their own, and significant things being moved when they normally remain untouched.

I once saw an apparition while bartending and thankfully, I wasn't alone because a friend of mine (who has his own history with spirits) noticed it too and told me to ignore it and 'let it go on its way.' Out of fear, I did, but it opened up the floodgates to a sense of wonder about the afterlife. I became convinced that unbeknownst to the rest of us, when people pass away, they still move about this Earth. Something about that idea filled me with peace.

One night at the bar, a friend of mine whose father had recently passed away wanted to take a shot in his honor. Our fathers had been friends back in the day and oddly enough, they had resembled each other when they were both alive: they had the same hair color and they both had beards. I remember as a child seeing his father around town and associating him to mine because of their similar appearances. As I poured a round, I told him how I used to compare our fathers when I was a kid. We laughed and took our shots, dedicating them to our deceased dads.

We continued talking and Ray, a new regular who had moved to Meadows and was now living next to the bar, overheard us and jumped into our conversation. Ray asked to see a picture of our fathers to judge whether or not they looked alike. I went into my wallet to retrieve one of my favorite pictures of my dad: him standing next to a lake, wearing a white fedora with beige pants and a white dress shirt, leaning on one side with his arms crossed, while holding a lit cigar. In this picture, my father looks very dapper and embodies swag. He looked to be in the prime of his life when that photo was taken. I carry it everywhere.

I begin to hold up the picture when Ray catches sight of it and his face drains. "That's your dad?"

I answer, "Yeah, why?"

He asked quickly, "When did he pass away?" He sounded scared.

I tell him the year. "Why?" I ask nervously, as he begins to pace back and forth. "You're freaking me out."

"Dude, I saw that guy standing by your car last week," he said.

My mouth dropped open. I am too stunned to speak but I manage to ask, "What?"

"I swear on my life. I was in the back smoking a cigarette and noticed this random man standing by your car, staring into the kitchen window," he insisted.

"Shut up," I deadpan with doubt, not believing him.

"Ellie, I swear on everything. I swear on my kids. On my mother. I saw that guy standing by your car, looking into the kitchen window," he said, firm in his statement. "Except, he was dressed differently. He was wearing jeans and a red shirt. The shirt had lettering on it."

In a majority of the pictures I have of my father, he is always wearing a work shirt (a red cotton tee with his company's name and phone number on it) along with dirty denim jeans. He wore that outfit Monday through Friday for many years. Ray couldn't have known that though because those pictures were in my mother's photo albums and I had never brought them to the bar. He also couldn't have known that my father was wearing that exact outfit the day that he had been attacked.

"You were working that night. Do you remember when you called out to me from the window because you heard me talking?" he asked. I actually did. I had been in the kitchen because I was making food and I heard Ray's voice. I called out to him to tell him to come inside.

"I was letting him know that I was watching him stand by your car. That's when you called out. I looked up at the window to respond to you and once I looked back up, he was gone. I thought it was weird but I forgot about it. Until just now." I waited for him to say he was joking, but he didn't. He was confident, concluding, "Your dad is here. He's watching you!"

I got chills at the thought...

*

Overtime, my friends started coming out to Harley's, which transitioned the bar from 'work' into a fun hotspot. For me, it became almost like a second home – the place I retreated to when I needed to 'get away' while at the same time, not wanting to be alone. My friends and I would get drunk off Jameson and we blended well with the rest of the people that corralled at Harley's. With good music blasting, Harley's became our safe haven and we made tons of memories between those walls.

It was a true transformation. I had started out working at Harley's looking down on it, and now I didn't think I belonged anywhere else. This bar, adorned with photos from the old days stapled onto the walls and streamers hanging from the ceiling, was now a place where I considered people I had once thought of as 'misfits', real friends.

I developed a deep connection to Harley's because my father had spent his twenties there just like I was. As I watched young fathers come to the bar and have a few drinks to get away from reality for a bit, I began to reexamine my father's choices and the resentment I had felt towards him. Perhaps he hadn't been ready to have a child, and the bar became a place where he could escape responsibility. Harley's forced me to stop looking at my father as if he were a mythical creature and realize that he had been a human being. It's because of this understanding that I was finally able to forgive him.

LA Woman

One of the most important people I have met from Harley's would have to be DJ. DJ and his friends had been coming into Harley's because he was close with Katie. DJ was ten years older than me and he had the kind of dry sarcasm that made you either laugh or feel stupid. For the first few weeks of me bartending in his presence, DJ remembers me as sitting on the beer box with a bitchy look on my face, "arms crossed, as if you wanted to be anywhere else in the world."

DJ was born and raised in New Jersey, but he had visited California in the 90's and eventually moved out there for good, residing in West Hollywood, a city in Los Angeles. He came back and forth to Jersey to visit, but he had no plans to move back because California was now his home. At the time, he was flying back and forth a lot on business, so during his down time he would visit the bar, a place where he could take a breather. I got the chance to really know him and began to look at him like an older brother-type. I appreciated that he treated me like a little sister as opposed to a prospect. He never hit on me and I liked that because it was rare at a place like Harley's.

One night, a friend of ours from the bar was having a party and I offered to drive DJ because his car was back in California. We drove through Jersey City to our friend's apartment and while sitting in traffic, he began to tell me stories of his experiences while living in Hollywood. DJ had seen some crazy things while working in the television industry and his stories made me yearn for an exciting life experience that would change my life for the better.

"I've always wanted to go to Hollywood," I sighed.

"Then you should," he said. "You can stay with me, I'll show you around. Book a flight."

"I can't just book a ticket. I would need to save money, I would need to prepare, I would need to-," I explained before he abruptly interrupted me.

"Nonsense. The first time I went to LA, I was broke. Once I got there, I never looked back," DJ persisted. "If you really want to go, you'll go. Here's your opportunity."

He was right – when would I have the chance to go to California with somebody who knew it inside and out again? With a little more convincing, I agreed. That night I left determined that by the next day, I would be booking a flight to the west coast. I knew my mother would balk at the idea of me going on vacation by myself, so I decided to beg Katie to go. I went to her house the next morning and bombarded her with the demand of us going to Los Angeles.

"Come on, we need to get away," I begged. It was the truth, we did. Too much work at Harley's and no play was making us boring girls. I convinced her to take a week off of work and we booked our tickets, right then and there, for a few weeks later. I was so excited I jumped around the room like a kid in a candy store.

We flew out of Newark and arrived at LAX. DJ was waiting for us by the baggage terminal and we gave him the happiest grins as we hugged him hello. When we were done retrieving our luggage, I ran outside to get my first real breath of California air.

The dry wind breezed by against the palm trees and since I had never seen a palm tree in person before, I bee-lined for the closest one so I could run my fingers against the wood. "What are you doing?" DJ asked, appalled.

"I've never seen a real palm tree in person!" I exclaimed.

"You look like a tourist. Act like you belong here," he said, smirking. "Oh, and not to burst your bubble, but California palm trees are actually imported from Florida." I curved my eyebrows in surprise hearing this.

We jumped in DJ's baby blue 71 Ford F100 truck that was parked at the LAX parking lot and zoomed on the freeway towards Hollywood. I stuck my head out of the window like a dog, exhilarated to be in California. I took pictures of everything; signs on buildings, oil pumps in the barren fields and of course, the infamous Hollywood sign.

Our first night there, DJ introduced us to some of his friends and we pre-gamed before we went out to the Viper Room. DJ's best friend was a bartender there, so we were treated like family from the second we walked in. We had a blast, taking tons of Jameson shots and we treated the night like it was our last one on Earth. Once the music stopped and the lights went on (surprisingly, bars in LA close at 2am), we retreated outside to figure out what else to do. There was quite the character outside, and being familiar with 'characters' from the bar, Katie and I were drawn to him almost immediately.

Next to a neon green vintage Cadillac was Dante, a flamboyant designer for a very popular clothing brand, known worldwide. "Ey, ey, where you pretty ladies headed?" he asked in broken English.

Katie, ever the socialist, stopped to talk to him, frustrating DJ who knew better than to fall for LA residents who preyed on cute tourists.

"We're outta here man, sorry," DJ said, putting his arm up to divide Katie and Dante.

Dante grinned. He was gay and he had no plans of trying to sleep with us. He really just wanted to show us a good time. "Let me give ya'll a ride home, or come to my house and we have an afta-party."

"I live right down the block. We don't need a ride," DJ said, pulling at our shirts as he began to walk. He looked back and noticed Katie's feet planted firmly on the ground, not budging. Me, I could have gone either way. I was drunk enough to go home and go to sleep, but not drunk enough where the idea of staying out was unheard of. Besides, it was our first night in Hollywood, so we wanted it to last as long as it could.

DJ stared at Katie.

"I'm going. I want to experience all random types of fun shit while I'm here. If I wanted to call it a night at 2am, I would have stayed in Jersey," Katie said, crossing her arms.

"Oh, my, God, so you ARE from Jersey! I knew it. Wonderful. Jersey girls are my favorite. They're just darling!" Dante screeched.

DJ looked at me who shrugged, and defeated, he exhaled a sharp breath and slowly walked back over to us.

"Wonderful," Dante said, clapping his hands. "Let's get going! We're going to have us a ball."

That we did. Dante took us for a long ride through the Hollywood Hills, full of dangerous winding roads and hillsides, where he showed us lavish celebrity homes. "That's Lindsay's house. The paparazzi camp out there all the time because she is allegedly dating that chick" and then, "Charlie Sheen crashed his car down that road." I already knew most of the trivia he told me since I was an avid-tabloid reader but I nodded eagerly as if he was bestowing knowledge upon me.

He drove onto Mulholland, where I finally got to see the glowing, star-filled location that was always shown on television; a purple sky against dark mountains and houses whose lights shined brightly. We drove past a cliff that overlooked a stunning view of Los Angeles, which DJ and Dante told me was commonly known as 'Make Out Point.' The lit-up scenery was magical – I felt lucky to see it in person.

We went back to Dante's house, still not ready to end our first night in LA, and I was stunned to see a real designer's home. His house on the outside was designed as a Spanish Revival house, with yellow stucco and painted tiles leading the way to a curved door under a wooden arch. Inside, the house was full of Andy Warhol paintings and life-size sketches of his designs next to crooked fashion awards on his walls. The neon pink walls against the zebra carpet proved his apartment was just as flamboyant as he was.

We sat around, engaging in drunk talk for a bit as we listened to Dante namedrop and brag about his career. Finally done with talking about himself, he put on house music and told Katie and I to try on some of his designs. I was elated when he handed me a dress he had made for an A-lister as he studied me carefully and said, "This would look terrific on you." He graciously asked us to be careful while wearing his designs and we promised we would. Katie and I had a mini fashion show complete with wardrobe changes as we pretended to be models in Louboutin heels that were too small, struggling to walk down the stairs to an amused DJ.

Katie, so-not-a-girly-girl, tripped in her heels and ripped the back of the dress that Dante had made for a client for an awards ceremony later that month. He winced in pain and put his head in his hands as he surveyed the damage. Looking for a way to cut the tension, Katie remarked that her glass was empty and it was time for a refill. All of a sudden Dante's face turned red and angry. She didn't notice and asked where the bottle of Jameson was.

"Clean the glass," he ordered, pointing a finger in her face.

"What?" Katie asked, confused and drunk. I looked at them nervously. DJ adjusted his glasses.

"CLEAN THE GLASS," he screamed, eliminating our

buzz.

Katie looked at him, almost amused. This guy was kidding, right? "Fuck you pal."

He began to scream and throw shit, barely missing my head with a coffee table book. Katie, a true Jersey girl in the sense that she was never one to back down from confrontation and on the contrary, she welcomed it, began to pick things up and throw them back at Dante. It became a war of flying objects, as DJ and I covered our heads while trying to inch towards the door. DJ, knowing this guy could be on anything, decided to get us out of there instead of retaliating so as Katie continued to scream back at Dante, DJ picked her up and threw her over his shoulder. We had never seen such unfounded rage and we couldn't stop laughing all the way off the property. We got to the street and as DJ set Katie on her feet, she threw her hands up in incredulity. DJ wiped the sweat off his head and exhaled.

"That was fun! Where's the closest diner?" she asked DJ, as if the last ten minutes hadn't happened.

Jersey had arrived.

*

The next day Katie and I, of course, did the tourist thing. We picked up some medical from a dispensary owned by one of DJ's friends and promptly rolled joints for each hour. We went to the Hollywood walk of fame, the Hollywood sign, and then later we had dinner at the Rainbow where we

165

were introduced to all of DJ's friends, including Diane, who offered to bring us to Venice Beach the next morning.

Diane picked us up early the next morning and we got to know her on our ride down the freeway. She was bubbly, charismatic, and outgoing and I knew right away that we had made another friend on the west coast. It was a beautiful sunny day. The three of us eagerly laid out on the beach and enjoyed the view: people riding their bikes on the boardwalk, tanned lifeguards reminiscent of Baywatch watching the ocean, and surfers doing what they do best against a background of mountains and palm trees.

We noticed paparazzi crowding around a group of girls on the beach and as I inched closer to get a view of who it was, one of the paparazzi started to film me with his camera. I had visions of me being Hollywood royalty like Paris Hilton and Nicole Richie with paparazzi following my every move so I promptly played it up for the camera, only to find out they weren't paparazzi at all, but cameramen for a Spanish news channel out in Mexico. It didn't matter to me – it was still exciting.

Lit from the medical, I felt on overwhelming surge of joy and Diane and Katie didn't even bat an eyelash when I ripped off my clothes down to my bikini and ran into the freezing-cold Pacific Ocean to dance by myself, in my own little world. Arms stretched out and hair blowing in the wind, I, for the first time ever, felt free.

"I don't think I've ever seen you so happy," Katie remarked when I came back, shivering cold but dripping happily with salt water. I hadn't either. I danced the rest of the time until it was time to leave.

*

The next day, DJ had a surprise waiting for me. He knew of my fascination with The Doors and he booked us a night at a motel where Jim Morrison had lived in Hollywood. Jim Morrison had lived there for some time while he was playing with The Doors and he had a habit of writing on the walls. The motel preserved the room after renovations and guests would stay in the room and write their own musings on the walls.

I could feel the vibe of Jim Morrison as soon as I opened the door. It was a basic motel room: a bed in the middle, sandwiched between two nightstands, a round table next to a window that overlooked Santa Monica Boulevard, a TV that appeared to be hanging by a mere wire, and a tiny bathroom with a stand-up shower.

Aside from that, this was no ordinary motel room: it had millions and millions of colorful writings on the walls. Poetry, song lyrics, quotes, and scattered thoughts painted every inch of the room, from the ceilings to inside the shower to inside the nightstand drawers. I had never seen anything like it. This place was a writer's dream.

After throwing our stuff on the bed, we promptly ran across the street to CVS to buy markers so we could scrawl on the walls too. After buying a pack in bulk, we raced back to the room, cracked open a bottle of Jameson and got to work. For a few hours, we sat quietly while listening to old Doors albums, writing on the walls and reading what other people have written.

Later on, DJ's friend came over and he brought a friend along. They were intrigued by the possibility of seeing the room that Jim Morrison once inhibited so they came bearing gifts: more medical, more booze, and In & Out Burger. A few hours later, we were sufficiently shit faced and we had an amazing time as we danced to Doors songs. As everyone else sang along and took pictures, posing against the various deep musings on the walls, I found an empty spot and scribbled:

"On this beautiful night, I am completely drunk with happiness…and drunk with Morrison. Thanks to my friends for experiencing this with me and to Jim, for being the quintessential icon of California. I <3 LA!"

Being in Jim Morrison's old room almost felt like a spiritual awakening. With dim lights and words surrounding me, I felt as though I had been thrown back into the seventies and was in the presence of Jim Morrison's ghost. Maybe I was crazy or maybe it was the medical, but I felt at one with that room, like I belonged there.

I fell asleep shortly after. The next morning, we woke up to DJ's friend who was in a near panic, opening the door. I rubbed my eyes and asked what was wrong.

"Xavier," he answered, referring to the friend he had brought over the night before, "He stole a car and he got locked up. He just called me from the police station."

That woke Katie up. "What?"

"Xavier stole a car."

"From where?"

"Melrose."

"Why the hell would he do that?" DJ asked.

"I would assume it was the drugs," DJ's friend answered frantically.

Katie and I looked at each other. Medical didn't seem like something that would push you to steal a car.

"What drugs?" I asked.

"Um, um, crack," he answered, embarrassed.

CRACK?! "When did he do crack?" I asked, horrified.

"Last night, when you guys were asleep, I caught him smoking it. I made him leave," he answered.

Katie began to laugh, these kinds of ridiculous things always amused her. "Wait, so he smoked crack, you kicked him out, and then he goes and steals a car?" she asked. DJ's friend nodded. "That's amazing."

We all looked at each other, not knowing what else to say. "Shall we go get breakfast?" DJ asked.

"We're going to leave him in jail?" I asked, concerned. I didn't know the guy and I didn't really want anything to do with somebody who smoked crack, but I was still worried about him.

DJ grabbed me by my shoulders, squeezing them, and winked. "Welcome to Hollywood, baby."

Californicated

You have to understand my obsession with celebrities and fame to really grasp why Hollywood was so fascinating to me. I grew up in a household where my mother spent ten dollars a week on tabloid magazines and spent most of her time watching entertainment television shows like E's *Talk Soup*. My fascination with fame started during the 1994 Olympics, when Nancy Kerrigan was attacked, and the media fully exploited it. My interest in fame (and it's ugly side) only grew from there.

Once Perez Hilton created a website about the daily goings of celebrities, at a time when Britney Spears was wearing pink wigs while talking in a British accent, I had aspirations of becoming one of the sought-after chicks who could raise thousands of dollars for a picture of them food shopping. The glorification of Paris Hilton, Nicole Richie, and

Lindsay Lohan's lifestyles made being a celebrity seem like it was something all chicks should aspire to be. The notion of free swag, paparazzi flashing cameras in your face, and getting paid to go to clubs seemed like an obvious desire for girls my age growing up in this era. It certainly was for me.

I knew I wouldn't be famous – I couldn't act or sing, and I didn't have the body nor the looks to be a model – but I still wished I could be. I dreamt that by going to LA, I would be discovered by talent scouts who would look at me and say, "That girl is meant to be a star" and then they would actually make me one. Thankfully, my ignorance was shattered once I was educated on the actual industry and not just the perks.

Two experiences during my first time in California humbled me. The first was during a show for a well-known band that was playing at a bar in the San Fernando Valley. Since DJ knew everybody in LA, we were given VIP passes which allowed us backstage. The backstage area looked worse-for-wear, but we noticed other people hanging around so as DJ stayed by the bar to hang with his buddies, Katie and I decided to make new friends.

Some time had passed, as well as a few joints, and before you knew it Katie and I were absolutely lit. We were beginning to feel out of place so we got up to leave as some band members walked in. They looked at us and clearly wondered who we were and why we were backstage, but they were in a rush to go somewhere so they grabbed their things and shut the door behind them.

I waited a minute to turn the knob to let us outside and as soon as I opened the door, I was blasted with flashing lights in my face. "CLICK!" "CLICK!" "CLICK!" There were at least six different cameras in my face, taking pictures, accompanied by blinding flashes. I froze in a stoned oblivion, not knowing what to do next.

Katie, behind me, laughed knowing how this normally would have thrilled me and whispered in my ear, "You want to be famous. Enjoy!" With that, she pushed me out the door.

I panicked – I was too lit to deal with flashes of the cameras and I stood there like a deer in headlights. Realizing these photographers were aggressive, I rushed back inside. I dialed DJ's number on my cell phone and pleaded with him to come retrieve us. I was shocked to witness first-hand how intrusive paparazzi were and I couldn't imagine how they behaved when they came across someone actually worthwhile.

"How was your first brush with fame?" Katie asked, teasing me.

"Definitely not what I thought it would be like," I answered. That was an understatement.

*

The next night I begged Katie and DJ to accompany me to a club that was famous for being a celebrity hotspot. DJ, annoyed, didn't want to go to a bar where he had to get dressed up. Up until then, we had mostly stayed on the 'rock' section of the Sunset Strip, where the Whiskey A Go Go, Rainbow Room and The Viper Room were. You didn't have to get dressed up for these places because they were casual rock bars and nobody cared what you wore – people were there for

173

music and a good time. In fact, if you did get dressed up, you were immediately considered 'trying too hard'. It was actually trendy to not be trendy.

Most of the celebrity hotspots in LA were down the road on Hollywood Boulevard. I desperately wanted to be able to hit up one of those clubs in the hopes of running into a celebrity and understanding my need to accomplish this goal while in Hollywood, Katie and DJ decided to go. Out of solidarity, they refused to dress up, but I did anyway, putting on my best bandage club dress.

We got to the club and the doorman looked us up and down. After a few minutes of Katie trying to sweet talk him into letting us in (not only were we not on the list, but my guests didn't exactly dress for a nightclub) he recommended we go to another bar around the corner. DJ became irate.

"Hey man, I know what you're trying to say," he accused.

"Oh? What is it that I'm trying to say?" the doorman asked innocently.

"You're calling us white trash."

"What?" I interrupted, thinking DJ was blowing our shot. "He didn't say that at all."

"That place is a hole in the wall dive bar. He doesn't think we're worthy to come into this bar because he thinks we belong there," he answered, getting even angrier. "I'm not a fuckin' tourist, I live here."

The doorman looked at DJ, who was wearing jeans, Converse sneakers and a black t-shirt, and then to Katie, who was wearing a plaid shirt with jeans and sneakers. I was the only one dressed up and with our strong Jersey accents, I couldn't really blame him for thinking we were 'not-up-to-par'. He was kind of right.

"If you live here, then you should know that this place," the doorman said, waving his hand as if to highlight the club, "requires a dress code nicer than sneakers and jeans." He looked at DJ with disgust.

Steam basically began to pour out of DJ's ears as he clenched his teeth and said, "You've got the wrong guy, pal." DJ may have been a resident of California, but he still had the Jersey attitude embedded in him. He wasn't going to be insulted and take it lightly. I sighed, frustrated.

The doorman didn't argue, he just ignored DJ and looked past him, waving in people behind us. As DJ and Katie started to argue over the insult of basically being called trash, I noticed a young boy with a huge camera waiting by the valet sign next to several paparazzi. I walked over to him, leaving Katie and DJ to rip the doorman a new one.

"What are you doing?" I asked the young boy, lighting up a cigarette. It was 11pm, this kid should have been home. 'Do kids in California not have curfews?', I thought to myself.

"Waiting for Paris and Kim to come," he answered matter-of-factly, gesturing towards his camera. He was, of course, referring to Paris Hilton, and her current best friend at the time, Kimberly Kardashian.

"Oh yeah?" I asked, looking around. "What are you going to do when they come?"

"Uh, take pictures of them?" he said, rolling his eyes, looking at me like I was an idiot.

I stared at him. This kid, with hair that resembled Justin Bieber's, had to be about 12 years old.

"You're a paparazzo?" I asked.

"Obviously," he challenged, before looking away.

"No way," I answered back, genuinely surprised. I had never known a kid to be a paparazzo, in fact, it was rare to even hear of women paparazzi. Men were the only ones bold enough to stalk and follow people in the pursuit of taking pictures. Or so I thought.

"Yeah, way." Skeptical, I asked him to prove it and with a smug look of determination, he began to go through his cell phone – a nicer, more technologically advanced phone than I had – and looked for a folder. Once he found it, he handed it to me and confidently said, "Scroll."

So I did. Imagine my surprise when I came across seriously impressive shots of reputable actors and actresses among other celebrities. "Wow," I said, still looking. "How do you find out where they are?"

"They tell me."

I looked at him and squinted my eyes. "What do you mean, they tell you?"

He sighed. "Look," he said, grabbing the phone from my hand to look through his text messages. He settled on one and showed me. The name on the message was that of a very well known celebutante. It was sent the night before and it was telling him that she would be at Le Deux that night around midnight. I scrolled up, just to make sure it wasn't a scam, only to find pictures he had taken of her sent to her and pleased responses back. She even sent him a selfie (before selfies were truly selfies) taken in her bathroom as she was getting her hair done by a stylist.

"She tells you where she goes?" I asked, my mouth dropping.

"Yup. They all do," he answered, popping his gum.

"But why? I thought celebrities hate being followed by paparazzi."

"That's what they want people like you to think," he laughed, probably thinking to himself what a dummy I was. "I have arrangements with them. A lot of celebrities tell paparazzi where they are going to be because they want the exposure."

He looked at me as if I should know this already. "They like me. They'd rather me make money than the creepy old guys that follow them. They think I'll put it towards college." He paused. "It helps that I give them half of what I get paid for the shots."

I was dumbfounded. All of those pictures of celebrities covering their eyes, hiding in their cars, and looking annoyed every time someone took their picture and here it was, all a ruse. The fame game was a scam! These celebrities were profiting off of their own invasions of privacy that they were asking for in the first place!

By this time, DJ and Katie were fuming after arguing with the doorman and they decided it was time to go back up the road to the Viper Room. I said goodbye to that young paparazzo, happy to go back towards the section of Sunset that didn't sell themselves out in exchange for profits and notoriety. We stopped by DJ's first so I could change out of my dress and into jeans and flip flops, and we went to our beloved, unpretentious rock bar...where we belonged.

Leaving On A Jet Plane

I loved California so much that I was on a natural high for a few weeks once we got back home. I felt as though I had seen a different part of the world and experienced something great so I was eager to get back. A few weeks after being home, I saved up enough money to buy tickets to go back in June. Katie wouldn't be able to come because she had to run the bar, so I decided I would go on my own. My mother was pissed, but it was too late, I had already bought my ticket and she knew that I wasn't going to take no for an answer.

This visit would be different from the first simply because a) it would be my second time on an airplane and my first time alone and b) during the week, DJ had to work so I would be on my own until the weekend. I was officially on an Ellie trip.

I was picked up at LAX by one of DJ's friends on his

work break and after handing me my own jar of Bubba Kush, he dropped me off to my own devices. Since DJ wouldn't be home until 8pm, he had left his keys under the doormat for me. I got inside, threw my bags on the couch and hit the pipe that Katie had left at DJ's when we had gone together. I decided to go for a walk and check out some stores to kill time before DJ got out of work.

While reading Star magazine, I had read about Robertson Boulevard, a street in Hollywood where celebrities went shopping and paparazzi roamed. DJ had told me in an earlier conversation that Robertson was 'a five minute walk' from his house. I knew the direction I had to go, so after taking a few more hits, I grabbed my bag and began to walk. It was time to shop.

DJ had clearly downplayed the distance. I had to walk all the way down the longest hill ever, also known as DJ's block. Then I had to cross over Santa Monica Boulevard and walk about eight blocks just to get into the heart of Robertson, where Kitson and the Ivy are. Now normally, this would have been an easy feat for me – but because I had mistaken the strength of the medical, I was suddenly smacked in the face with a massive, stupefying high. Even worse, I had no direction whatsoever and I was alone. I needed a pick-me-up so I stopped walking in a daze down the street and stopped in a Starbucks, ordering a caramel macchiato.

After asking the cashier for directions, I continued on my walk and stopped in front of The Ivy, an Italian restaurant where celebrities ate when they wanted to be seen because the paparazzi were always around. Still lit, I sipped my coffee when all of a sudden, a crowd of twenty men enveloped me with cameras. I jumped up out of shock, suddenly consumed with clarity, and promptly spilled coffee all over my shirt.

A man was now in front of me and being pursued by paparazzi. He had used me as a type of shield unsuccessfully, and now I was in the background of his shot, spilling coffee all over myself. He looked back at me sheepishly, as if to apologize, and it was then that I realized it was one of the singers in a well-known boy group that was popular at the time. As he continued to appear like he was trying to dodge these middle-aged men following him, he was chatting with them the whole time. I stared for a moment, stunned to see this guy in real life. He was actually a lot shorter than I had imagined.

I was embarrassed by the coffee stain on my shirt, so I ran into the nearest gas station to get paper towels and water from the restroom to wipe off, only to see the boy band member come into the gas station too. As I waited in line behind him, I couldn't help but notice the paparazzi outside, shoving their elbows into each other while yelling his name. The way these men were acting about getting videos and pictures of him in the gas station, you would have thought it was Brad Pitt next to me. The glass continued to shake against the paparazzi fighting and I noticed the cashier getting visibly concerned. "Geeze," I muttered to myself under my breath, rolling my eyes.

He sensed the annoyance, looked over at me, and tilted his heads towards them. "Ridiculous, right?" he asked. I nodded. It really was. Still, he didn't look too bothered by it, and I wasn't surprised when we walked out of the gas station together and he ignored the blinding camera flashes in his eyes to start a friendly chat with the paparazzi once again. I scattered away, relieved that I was out of eyeshot.

The rest of the week was filled with star sightings, as I met Dave Navarro outside of Hustler on Sunset and ran into Kat Von D at The Rainbow Room. I also ran into a high profile actress at The Viper Room, only to be disappointed when I realized that despite playing a friendly girl on her hit TV show, she was actually not one in real life. A legendary comedian nearly hit me with his sports car on Hollywood Boulevard and instead of apologizing, he cursed me off. I swore I'd never watch any of his stand up specials again because regardless of the fact that he was hilarious, he was an asshole in real life.

Being up close and personal with people I had seen onscreen and gawked over in magazines was eye opening as I realized that these celebrities were normal people, just like me. Surprisingly, I found that disappointing. The allure of celebrity was diminishing. I had always wanted to be famous and now that I had a little more insight, I changed my mind. I was actually cool with just being me.

*

I ended up staying the rest of the week with Diane and her girlfriends at Le Montrose off of Sunset, and we had a blast enjoying the pool and living it up. I lived it up so much that after lying in the hot summer sun (and like an idiot, using baby oil as a tanning oil), I developed sun poisoning and had to spend the entire day rubbing potatoes all over my body and staying out of the sun. Thankfully, Diane took care of me, and I was ready the next day to go back out and enjoy everything else that Los Angeles had to offer.

Los Angeles brought beautiful things into my life, but the most important aspect were the new people I met. Being stuck in Meadows all of my life, all I knew was who I grew up with and those I had met along the way. I was a goldfish in a suffocating bowl with other goldfish that knew only exactly what I knew. But that was it – we all had our limits of experience – and in that little fish bowl, there was no way to grow.

Thankfully, DJ had tons of friends from literally everywhere and he didn't mind sharing them. Through him, I was able to meet people from Japan, South Carolina, Washington, and other various places. I made friends with people who were older than me, who had more life experience than I did, and it was through their eyes and perspectives that I learned a little bit more about life on that trip. I soon found another loyal group of lifelong friends.

*

My last morning in California, before everybody woke up, I went for a walk on Runyon Canyon, an infamous scenic trail in Hollywood. I wanted a moment to myself and I knew that settling in the top of the mountains alone would not only be peaceful, but therapeutic as well.

I didn't expect a sudden fear of heights that would

develop as soon as I got closer to the top of the canyon and I instantly began to regret my decision of walking so far up. As I panted and avoided looking over the sides of the cliff, I walked up the painfully steep trail, and wondered if I had been crazy to do this excursion by myself. If I fell over the side, who would know where I was to look for me? As joggers and their dogs sprinted past me with an impressive no-fear attitude, I began to literally crawl up the trail, fingers digging into the dirt, in hopes I wouldn't get knocked over.

By the grace of God, I made it. As I settled on the highest point of the canyon, Los Angeles waking up beneath me, the adrenaline in my blood hit its maximum and I plopped on a bench, overlooking the city. I sat there for about an hour, enjoying what would be one of the most peaceful experiences of my life, nature and universal opportunity surrounding me as the sun shined down on my face.

*

Of course, as soon as I got home from that trip, I was ready to go back. Life back at home in Meadows was now so boring to me. I was working a lot and my friends were doing their own thing. I felt a different kind of liveliness in California and I wanted to embrace it as much as I could - so Katie and I saved up and we bought flight tickets to go back in August, my third time in six months.

Our first day back in California was, of course, instantly exciting of epic proportions. DJ picked us up from LAX and we immediately went to a western-themed dive bar to have some happy hour drinks and get our vacation started right. We ran into a couple of people that DJ knew, including Zane, a guy with ear gages so big you could put your fist through them.

We ordered drinks and some shots. The bar had a huge mechanical bull in the center of the room and DJ suggested I try it. I lasted about three seconds before I was thrown onto the safety mat underneath the bull. It was hysterical and it set up our time as a good one...until the checks came.

Zane's friends, who had ordered several beer towers way before we got there and tons of food, had a bill amounting to $500. We had a separate check, so we paid our bill and started to get up. We looked around, but Zane had already left and his friends were nowhere to be found, so we figured we would see them on our way out. As we hit the exit, the manager stopped us.

"Excuse me, you have to pay that check," the manager ordered.

DJ looked around and realizing the manager was speaking to us, asked, "What check?" The manager gestured towards our table.

"You've made a mistake buddy, we paid our bill," DJ said, beginning to walk away.

"Sir, if you leave, we are calling the police. Nobody paid for the other check." He was referring to Zane's check.

"That was our friends bill," DJ answered, as if this were common sense.

"Yes, and your friends left, so somebody needs to be held responsible for it."

"WE paid for what WE ate and drank. We're leaving,"

185

DJ answered, insisting we walk. Katie and I looked at each other and followed behind him, while the manager and waitress yelled. We caught a slight glimpse of Zane's friends running up towards the canyon and as we screamed their names, they acted as if they couldn't hear us and disappeared into the shrubs.

We walked about a block before the cops were pulling up to us and putting us in handcuffs. Katie understandably resisted and the cop shoved her face into the door as she was detained. DJ roared, how could we be held responsible for somebody else's tab? I was terrified - I knew that if I had to call my mother from a jail in California, I was never going to be able to come back again.

To make matters even worse, DJ and Katie were put into the same cop car while I was put into another one, alone. We started to drive until I noticed the cop car with DJ and Katie eventually slow down. I tried to adjust myself to see what they were doing and I sharply exhaled when I saw the cop letting DJ and Katie out of the cuffs.

"What's going on?" I cried to the cop.

"Let me see," he answered, getting out of his car to go talk to the cop letting DJ and Katie go. They exchanged some words and eventually, the cop strolled over to me.

"You're free to go," he said, opening the door and releasing my handcuffs. As I scooted over to get out, I observed DJ standing there with a furious look on his face. I ran over to DJ and Katie, hugging them.

"What the hell?" I asked, still shaken.

"Since Zane's friends ran out on the tab, I had to pay

the exact amount in order for the cops to let us go. Those scumbags just cost me half of my rent!" DJ said angrily.

Katie and I stood there in silence - we knew we couldn't help DJ because we had limited funds for the week we were there.

He noticed the look on our faces and assured us, "Don't worry, Zane is going to give me the money. If not, I'm kicking their asses." He squinted his eyes towards the sun. "Where do you guys want to go now?"

It was typical DJ – the world could be going through the apocalypse and he just wanted to have fun regardless. We continued walking to get more drinks, relieved.

"Can you believe that cop slammed my head into the cop car? He's lucky I don't sue his ass!" Katie said.

Our first three hours back in California and we had already been shoved into a cop car and threatened with arrest. Jersey was back.

*

This time, DJ had taken off a day or two to spend time with us, but for the most part, he was going to be at work. Katie and I rented a car so we could explore different parts of LA and not die of heatstroke while doing so. We rented a little white Rav-4 in the Valley and set off onto more adventures. Having a car brought much broader options and we took advantage almost immediately, running to get In & Out Burger and driving through the hills to the Griffith Observatory, overlooking the city. It's one of my favorite moments, just me and my best friend, driving around and enjoying life.

We visited Santa Monica (we almost died of horror when we noticed people going into the ocean with soap) and Malibu, which we both agreed was stunning. The next day we were off to Venice Beach, where we laid on the beach for hours getting lit. "I never want to go home," Katie would say, stretching out her arms and grazing the sand. I sighed, wishing we didn't have to. California was becoming my favorite place on Earth.

The rest of the week we drove all around Los Angeles together and we made a new friend one day who brought us to an exclusive club. Finally, I was going to a hotspot which just so happened to be hosting a red carpet event that night!

Katie and I wore our one and only 'club' outfits that I insisted we pack; short dresses with high heels, "just in case". We mingled, danced, and enjoyed ourselves so much that we began to feel euphoric. After leaving the club, we met up with DJ and his friends at a bar on the Strip. Before we knew it, we were trashed and it was time to end our night. We stumbled on the Strip on our way back to DJ's and I threw up on a side street, much to the horror of those driving by.

I wish I could describe more of that night, but I can't; somebody had slipped roofies in both of our drinks and neither of us remembered a damn thing. We didn't go far – DJ found us on his couch with our dresses still on, asleep and snoring. It could have ended up much worse but we were lucky.

Hollywood, baby.

*

In those three times of visiting California over the course of several months, never once did I seek out any company from guys in the hopes of a vacation fling. My friends back in Jersey were appalled when I would come home with stories that didn't include any new guys. "No suitable guys out there, just rich and handsome ones, huh?" they would joke. "No stories for us?! What a waste." They were shocked. They didn't get it – going to California wasn't about finding a guy out there – it was about finding myself.

Mission accomplished.

Karma Chameleon

Life, eventually, comes full circle. Back when I was in seventh grade, I had an embarrassing obsession with a senior in the high school named Jeffrey. Jeffrey resembled Leonardo DiCaprio and he dressed like a guy who cared about the way he looked. He always appeared remarkably put together and stood out against a sea of Abercrombie & Fitch-wearing teenagers. With eyes the color of sky blue Crayola crayons, sandy blonde hair, and a voice that reminded me of love songs, I was smitten.

Everyone in my grade knew about my crush and would give me updates every time Jeffrey walked the halls. Whenever he would stroll past me so unknowingly handsome, I would hyperventilate, clutching my chest and choking on my own breath. To see me react this way in front of people was funny and made everyone around me laugh, but for the wrong reasons. Keep in mind, this was the year before I gained notoriety as "Ellie Belly". Not only was I getting fat, but I would also act like a complete moron every time this ordinary teenager went about their day.

Eventually my 'crush' turned into semi-stalking. I would call his job and giggle when he would answer, hands cupping the telephone so my muffled laugh wouldn't be recognized, and hang up once he sounded like he was getting frustrated. I walked past his house everyday after school even though it was out of my way, in hopes I would see him walking in or out the front door. When I did manage to catch a sight of him, I would run and hide.

Maybe I was a little too overeager and aggressive. One day I ran into Jeffrey's best friend while walking in the mall. He looked at me and barked, "I'm going to make Jeffrey get a restraining order on you! Leave him alone!" My heart crushed and I was instantly devastated. Why did this kid care if I liked Jeffrey? He sounded jealous, but why? Still, his message was loud and clear. Even at that age, I knew I had to show some form of pride so from that point on, I never spoke of Jeffrey again.

Until...

Aside from working at Harley's, I started working weekends at a banquet hall as a bartender, working open bar for weddings and other events. One night, while working a wedding, I had a moment in between cocktail hour and the reception to sneak out and have a cigarette on the side of the building where workers went to have a smoke. As I lit up my cigarette, I felt the presence of somebody near by, watching me. I looked over and there was Jeffrey, dressed in a formfitting gray suit and looking as fine as ever, smoking a cigarette mere inches away.

By this time, I looked very different from the little girl he knew of years and years ago but he remembered me. He smiled his megawatt smile and walked closer to me. I blushed and smiled back, digressing back to being a shy seventh grader who wanted to run and hide.

Accompanied by a grin, he said, "Hi! I remember you. Ellie, right? You've grown up, huh? You're beautiful," he said. For a split second, the teenager in me silently yelled, 'Victory!'

Then, the words no former tween stalker wants to hear,

"How did you not know I was gay?"

Oh.

Then,

duh.

This guy, who I basically stalked as a teenager, who had been 'everything' to me, who I had dreamt upon stars to have this moment come true as adults, with nothing holding us back...was gay. The more he talked, the more embarrassed I was that I had never realized it before.

As he told me, Jeffrey was at the banquet hall because he was in the wedding party and he was trying to sneak a cigarette between taking pictures with the bride and groom. We continued our conversation and I briefly mentioned his best friend from high school who had traumatized me by yelling at me. Jeffrey rolled his eyes, "He wasn't my best friend. We were secretly dating." Of course, now it made sense!

The rest of the conversation proved that while Jeffrey may have been larger than life to me when I was a seventh grader, he wasn't really extraordinary nowadays. He had moved to Maine and had a normal life there. He was typical and ordinary, but still as hot as he used to be. Gay men were definitely lucky to have this guy in their dating pool and I found myself hoping we could keep in touch, even if was just on Facebook.

Before we parted ways, Jeffrey turned to look at me one last time. Making an all-knowing face he said,

"Just so you know, if I was straight, I would totally fuck you."

*

My last year in college and for the first time ever in my life, I am considered 'hot'. Not pretty, not cute, but hot. My body is thin, my long hair is envy inducing, and I have realized the magic in bronzer. Knowing guys look at me as a 'hot girl' gratifies me in a self-affirming way and I began to believe them.

Since I am in my own final year in college, most of the people who considered me Ellie Belly are already back at home. If they haven't obtained their dream careers or gotten married, they, more often than not, reunite with their high school buddies at the local bars. Not only out of boredom, but because they don't know how to be around people who don't consider them one of the 'cool' kids from high school. They are the new townies.

When I first started bartending at Harley's, one of my main concerns was having to serve drinks to people who tortured me while growing up. Running into my bullies reminded me of my teenage mindset, vulnerable and timid, and I hated feeling that way. Since I couldn't control who came into the bar and who didn't, when those kinds of situations happened I had no choice but to suck it up and serve them with a smile.

The night Kyle Hall walks into Harley's, my stomach drops and my heart begins to race. I am immediately thrown back to being an eighth grader who is afraid to look him in the eye out of fear that it will trigger him into teasing me. I search for Katie, who is nowhere to be found, and I know I have no choice but to face him head on because I can't avoid him. I have to serve him. It pains me – but I do it.

"Hey, what will it be?" I ask casually, as if the mere sight of him doesn't derail me and my confidence into oblivion.

He looks at me with bloodshot eyes and I watch him study my face. I crack a smile to myself once I realize that this idiot is too fried to remember me. I sigh with relief and act normal.

"Let me get a scotch on the rocks," Kyle says. I comply and engage in polite small talk until Katie pops up and comes over to catch up with Kyle. Once I have a reason to walk away, I do, all the while noticing Kyle's eyes on me, wondering why I look so familiar.

Over the course of my shift, Kyle stays and continues checking me out, studying my body as I lean against the beer cooler. "Would you want to hang out sometime?" he asks, fingering the top of his glass.

"You don't remember me, do you?" I ask.

He studies my face, squinting his eyes. He shook his head. "I kind of do..." He laughs, "Did we go to school together?"

"Yes," I state, simply.

"You went to Meadows High?"

"Yep."

"I think I would remember you."

"Does Ellie Belly ring a bell?" I ask, point blank.

His eyebrows bend and after several awkward minutes, he remembers and says, "Holy shit, you're, like, hot now."

I stare at him, hiding the furious steam aching to release from my ears. I act indifferent, but hearing him compliment me angers me. I appreciate compliments, but not from him.

"So what, you hate me? I was a kid back then too. What did I know?" he reasons. I cross my arms.

"Let me make it up to you," he presses.

I push away the glasses that are between us and lean towards him, folding my arms on the wooden bar top. He leans in excited because he has the wrong idea. I whisper into his ear with my raspy, sometimes unintentionally sultry voice, "No-fucking-way."

He backs away, looking crushed, and says, "I understand."

Clearly Kyle doesn't understand because over the next couple of months, he will come into Harley's during every single shift I work. He will buy me shots in the hopes that I get drunk, eventually let my guard down, and give him a chance to redeem himself. It doesn't work. He goes out of his way to try to make me un-hate him with his charm. The scary thing is, that does work.

Kyle and I end up hanging out together with a few mutual friends and he eventually brings me around the crew that picked on me in middle school, the 'Co.' in Kyle & Co. These guys that had been popular, good-looking jocks were now out of shape, miserable with their spouses, and drug addicts. Like flies to shit, they flock over to me, and act as if we are old friends. 'This is it,' I think to myself. 'This is the moment all of those tortured high school movies aim for.' As I avoid the hungry looks in their sunken eyes, I stay strong and hold my own, knowing that these guys regret bullying me because now they find me worthy.

During the many times we hang out, Kyle will admit that life after high school hadn't been as awesome as he thought it would be. Once at college, nobody seemed to care if he was the Big Man On Campus back at Meadows because there were thousands of good looking, athletic guys who made him fade into obscurity. Far away from home and since all of his friends had gone their separate ways, he was, for the first

197

time ever, on his own.

I was sympathetic to him feeling alone, because I knew that feeling all too well. Kyle eventually wins me over as a friend and I begin to overlook the past and appreciate the person he is now, even if he is relentless in pursuing me. He begs me to change my mind only to be turned down because he impacted my spirit too much for me to look at him in that kind of way. I will never give him a chance and he knows it, but that doesn't stop him from trying.

One night Kyle invites me over to a friend's house who was having a barbeque. I went, and after many hours of drinking in the sun, I realize it's time to go home. I try to sneak out but Kyle catches me. I insist on him staying put with his friends but he demands on walking me out, shadowing two steps behind me the whole time. This was the first time Kyle and I were in each other's company alone, drunk, and I had a knot in my stomach. 'Ugh', I think to myself, 'He's definitely going to try to kiss me.'

As I turn around to say goodbye, Kyle swoops in like a falcon, leaving me no time in between him grabbing my face and suffocating me for me to pull away. Instantly his tongue is in my mouth and I can hear the teenager in me cryptically yelling, 'Don't do this!'

As I begin to resist, I notice something: his tongue is licking my teeth instead of dancing around with my own tongue. His tongue never leaves my teeth and I realize that Kyle, the most popular guy in town who used to bully me and made me suicidal, is a bad kisser.

I burst out laughing and we pull away, him looking

disappointed and me looking relieved. I give him a kiss on the cheek and say goodbye, sprinting to my car as soon as his shadow leaves and he goes back to his friends.

My heart beats fast as I realize what has just happened and instantly, I throw up everywhere. On the curb, on my shoes, on my car door. I want to cry, but instead I continue to laugh.

My mother had been right that one night...the guy who used to torture me ended up kissing the ground I walked on. At that moment, it occurred to me how things change and you don't realize it until moments like that. I got in my car, driving away content.

Ellie Belly was officially dead.

One Way Out

My favorite band was playing a show in New York City, so I went with a group of friends and we made it into a daylong adventure. We hopped on the bus, took a train, and ended up a few blocks away from the venue. We decided to get lunch and then bar hop for a bit, eventually tumbling in to see the show.

Once the show was over, we went to the venue's lobby to hopefully catch a glimpse of the band. The lead singer was, at first, noticeably absent but he eventually came out and graciously took pictures with our group, his arm a little too tight across my shoulders. Just as soon as he had appeared, he disappeared. The night was over, or so it seemed.

We all looked at each other and wondered what to do next, our eyes settling on the hotel across the street that had one of the city's hottest bars inside. Without saying a word, we set off to go have a few more drinks before heading home.

Once inside the bar, we ordered a round of drinks and a few minutes later, I noticed The Singer come in without anybody realizing who he was. I realized that he was probably staying at this hotel for the night because the band was on tour. About an hour later, I was walking to the bathroom when The Singer bumped into me and spilled some of his beer on my shoulder.

"Oh shit, sorry!" he said, jumping back.

I looked down and shrugged it off, telling him, "No worries. Hey, your show was great before!"

"Thanks for saying that. I get nervous up there sometimes. New York City is a tough crowd." He smiled, a twinkle in his eyes. Swoon!

"No problem," I responded, not knowing whether to continue towards the bathroom or take advantage of these few minutes of chatting with the lead singer of my favorite band.

"What are we going to do about your shirt?" he asked.

"It's okay, I'm going home soon," I answered, nodding towards my friends across the bar.

He looked at me surprised, "Most chicks would be trying to get something out of me by now."

I waved it off, "Not me."

"I have some tour shirts in my room if you want one. I'll give you a few extra for your friends to make it up to you for the inconvenience," he offered. "My room is on this floor, your friends probably won't even notice you're gone."

I looked over to my friends who were oblivious to the fact that I was talking to The Singer while they were ordering Jameson shots. "Okay." I had to pee anyway. "Can I use your bathroom too?'"

He put his arm out, and surprised by the gesture, I gave him a look before wrapping my arm around his. Was this really happening? I figured that at the least, I would be able to tell my grandkids I ran into this guy, entailing a good story one day.

We walked and made small talk on where to get the perfect New York City slice of pizza. He opened the door to his suite and it was absolutely stunning, accelerating anything I've ever seen in person. The room was huge and decorated so modern that I felt like I was in a ritzy Beverly Hills hotel room. The bathroom was nothing short of a suite within itself, separated into two parts: a room with the toilet and a glam room. It was perfect, fit for a queen, and not to mention a waste, since this guy was living out of a small suitcase that pathetically stood next to the closet door. I doubt he took advantage of the antique claw bathtub.

The Singer rummaged through a cardboard box and grabbed a black t-shirt with his tour title emblazoned on the front, tossing it to me before motioning where the bathroom was. I bee-lined for the bathroom, peed, and changed my shirt. It was baggy on me and made out of scratchy material, but I kept it on anyway.

When I walked out, The Singer, posing semi seductively on the couch with his arms stretched out, glanced at me and said, "My shirt looks good on you." It was the kind of shirt that never looks impressive on girls, but I blushed hearing this anyway.

As I mentioned it was probably time for me to get back

to my friends, he nodded and got up. Upon opening the door, he closed it back shut and began to kiss me, grabbing the back of my neck while pulling me in.

In the one minute we made out, this was my thought process:

Second 1: Whoa.

Second 2: Okay.

Second 3: What?

Second 5: What?!

Second 7: Hmmm...definitely a decent kisser.

Second 10: Is this really happening right now?

Second 15: He's kind of old.

Seconds 16-30: But a really decent kisser.

Seconds 31-40: I mean, he's not THAT old. It's not like he's nursing-home-old.

Second 41: He's definitely like 15-20 years old than me.

Seconds 42-50: (Does The Math)

Second 51: Yep, he is old.

Second 52: This is weird.

Second 53: But cool.

Second 54: (Second-guesses the math, does the math again, still old.)

Second 57: A few more seconds and I'm done.

Second 60: (I pull away)

Second 61: That just happened.

He looks at me quizzically. "I'm sorry, but I'm sure my friends are waiting to go home and I'm probably holding them up and they are probably looking for me so I-," I ramble.

"Wait," he says.

Then – just when I thought my night couldn't get any better – it did.

"Can I jerk off to your feet?" he asked nonchalantly, as if he had asked me to pass the butter.

My jaw dropped to the ground. Did the lead singer of my favorite band just ask to jerk off to my feet? I waited for him to add in, "Just kidding." He didn't.

I stood in shock for a moment and then made my grand escape, giving him a sympathy hug and I left, with a frozen 'what-the-hell' face.

"I'll call you!" he yelled as I made my still-stunned exit. No he wouldn't. He didn't have my number.

'My phone!', I realized. I checked my phone, and sure enough, I had several missed calls and texts. I returned to my friends who were pissed off that I hadn't answered my cell phone in the time I had gone MIA, who eventually burst into hysterics once I explained the singer-who-wanted-to-masturbate-to-my-feet story. "That kind of shit could only happen to you," they said, "Seriously." We laughed until our stomachs hurt.

Now every time his name comes up, like when he performs or puts out a new album, everyone asks me the same thing:

"What kind of shoes were you wearing?"

The Past Should Stay Dead

I began dating a family member of a good friend of mine, Damien. He was successful, more than financially stable, and literally a sweetheart, inviting me over to find my favorite candy displayed out on the table. He was perfect on paper: gentle, sweet, and romantic – literally everything a girl could want in a guy. For a short while, I had him... but he came into my life at the worst time.

My grandfather learned he had cancer a few months before I graduated college. He took a turn for the worst and ended up getting admitted into a local hospital where my family took turns visiting him and caring for him. The reality that the patriarch of our family was breathing his last few breaths was harsh and our family dynamics shifted enormously because of it.

One day, after numerous times of refusing, I decided to go see my grandfather in the hospital one day with my mother after class. We spent the entire car ride in silence and somberly parked in the levels, holding hands as we walked into the hospital, knowing that this could be the last chance I could have to see my grandfather alive. The sharp smell of disease and death filled the hallways, masked by Glade air freshener, and I tried hard to hold my nose until we got into his room.

My mother knocked on the door, and he weakly yelled, "Come in." We walked in. My grandfather, or this body that was once known as my grandfather's, was sprawled out on the hospital bed, tubes coming out of his skin from all directions. My once chubby grandfather was now as skinny as a toothpick. I froze – I had never seen somebody so discombobulated in the flesh before and I was scared that merely speaking out loud would break him – so I said nothing.

He noticed my unusual silence and tried to break it. "Why the hell are you being so quiet? What's wrong with you?" he asked.

"I-I-," I stuttered. My mother began to fix the pillows behind his head and they both looked at me, giving me looks that demanded me to pretend everything was normal. I couldn't – I have a serious inability to hide my emotions – so I excused myself and went to the bathroom, locking the door and catching my breath. Once I was in, I dropped to my knees and began to quietly sob, stuffing the moans down to my stomach, not daring to let them be heard.

I collected myself and went back out, forcing a conversation with my grandfather as we watched a football game on the tiny TV above the cabinet. We discussed college and after catching me fixate on the tattoo on his arm, the one I used to gingerly touch with my stubby fingers as a child, he ordered me to never get any tattoos. "Okay," I assured him, not having the heart to tell him I had gotten my first tattoo, a star on my ankle, years ago.

He died a few days later. There was a wake, proudly decorated in American flags for his service in the military, and he was buried in the same cemetery as my father.

As close as I had been to my grandfather, I felt disconnected from the loss of him. After coming to terms with my experience of death with my father, I had an indifferent attitude towards people passing away. Losing another father figure didn't matter because I had already lost one already. I mourned his death differently, losing myself in my head-phones during the hours in between viewings, as everyone around me cried.

*

My mother succumbed to stress and depression. Not coping with my father's death properly and now having to deal with her own father's death became too much for her, and there were days she couldn't even get out of bed. I tried everything in my power to make her happy – but depression doesn't work that way. It took a long time for me to understand that I couldn't fix her.

I contemplated life a lot once my mother began to unravel. What was the point of living this life – where I had done everything right; not getting pregnant as a teenager, not becoming a drug addict and graduating college on the Deans

List, if my mom wasn't happy at the end of it all? I did everything right, I hadn't become another statistic of girls with 'daddy issues', yet I still ended up with hardships.

Knowing that my mother felt unfathomable depths of pain was hard to understand and I felt my own enormous amount of sadness because I couldn't do anything to help her. Nothing hurts more than watching the person you love the most hurt beyond measure. I had to stuff these feelings down when I was around other people but when I was alone, I disintegrated.

*

My mother used to call me Empathetic Ellie, because of my nature of being way too concerned with how people felt. As a child, when I found homeless kittens on Paper Street, I begged my mom to let me keep them so I could care for them in a way they deserved and I cried for hours when she refused. Every Halloween as an elementary student, I donated all of my allowance to UNICEF, proudly dropping dollar bills into the little orange boxes. As a teenager going into the city to drink underage with the girls, I would pass by homeless people and go into nearby delis and buy them food to eat, leaving only a few dollars to enjoy myself. I didn't want praise, I just wanted to help because my heart ached for them.

I spent most of my life worrying about people and once I was thrown into new territory where the person who was suffering was my own mother, I found a type of responsibility on my shoulders that I wasn't ready for yet. I became annoyed, resentful, and angry. In my words to my mother many times, "Why can't you just be happy?" I screamed, I cried, and I made my mother's depression about me. In return, instead of helping solve the problem, I became a problem.

All of the beauty and wonder in the world suddenly turned ugly. The life in me was sucked out dry. I became a bit of a chaotic, nervous wreck and Damien and my friends sensed it. I withdrew, not answering phone calls or going out, becoming isolated as a recluse in my own personal messed up life. Damien tried to keep in touch for a while, but eventually he gave up. I couldn't blame him – I had become a shell of the person I once was.

My life sucked.

But then....

I met Jax…

and **everything** changed.

I met him on an ordinary night.

I didn't expect to meet **the love of my life**, then and there.

When he walked in the door, the energy in the room shifted.

Our eyes locked.

I was changed.

I was impacted.

I looked at him…like nobody else existed.

And I

never wanted to look into another mans eyes again.

I had found him.

My knight in shining armor.

My handsome prince.

He was perfect.

He was everything.

Except,

he was married.

Edge Of Seventeen

It was a regular night at Harley's and I was trying to keep my mind off of things by enjoying the music and staying busy. The Ipod was blasting Kings of Leon for a good three hours until Katie took notice and changed it, wanting to play something else. A bunch of our friends were out that night and I was happy to see my friend Ben walk in. I was even happier when I noticed the hot friend he had brought in with him. My stomach flip-flopped and my cheeks heat up. His friend was wearing a white t-shirt with black Buddy Holly glasses and he was sexy. Really sexy.

I remember having the thought that this person was going to influence my life in a major way but I ignored it, eager to be introduced. I bee-lined towards them and asked them what drinks they wanted. As Ben introduced me to this person who I knew was now named Jax, I locked eyes with him. I was instantly drawn to him, almost as if I was magnetized. As he began to talk, I focused on his lips, and thought to myself how smooth and inviting they looked.

I made their drinks, all the way side-looking Jax. He acted like he didn't notice me staring at him as he explored the bar, looking at the pictures on the wall and playing with Katie's guitar. I excitedly whispered to her, "Oh my God, isn't that guy Jax so cute?" She looked at him and shrugged, implying he was not her type, but I was still intrigued.

After doing my rounds and making sure my customers got their refills, I noticed Jax was still playing with Katie's guitar, strumming chords. I complimented him on how well he was playing to which he quietly said, "Thanks." He was so shy, something unheard of to me. Everyone I knew was outspoken, including myself.

I took Ben to the side and asked, "What's his deal? He's so cute!"

"He's married," Ben deadpanned. My stomach dropped to the floor. I didn't even realize that Jax had a ring on his finger...which made me further realize I never had to look for a ring because most guys I knew were not married.

"What? How old is he? He looks so young."

"He's 23," he answered. I nodded slowly but in my head I thought to myself, who the hell gets married at 23? I was the same age and I was nowhere near marriage. I was bummed but I left it alone, trying to ignore the obvious attraction I felt.

*

That night I had a dream where I was in an apocalyptic

version of Meadows that was transformed into an abandoned carnival, with all sepia-like colors. The buildings in the distance had sheets blowing in the windows and in the middle of town was a shaky and creaky ferris wheel, but I still wanted to go for a ride. I got on and once I sat down, the ride started to go much faster than it had been going before. I begin to panic and look for a way off, as my hair starts whipping in the wind. My fingers clenching the sides, I search my surroundings for any signs of life when I notice Jax standing in the distance.

I start to relax at the sight of him and begin to call his name as he strolls towards me with ease. He pushes a button at the bottom and the ride slows down towards him. As I begin to stand up to get off the ride, Jax surprises me by getting in and sitting next to me. Looking at him, I push the button and the ride starts up again, as the scenery changes to a blue sky and lush green trees. I wake up relieved, yet disappointed, that it was all just a dream.

*

"Look him up on Facebook," Christina casually offered the next day, after I described my dream to her.

"For what? He's married. I'm not doing that," I replied, appalled at her selfishness. Why the hell would I look him up on Facebook? What would be the point?

"You're not doing anything wrong, everyone is friends on Facebook these days," she reasoned. Christina had been hooking up with a guy who had a girlfriend and she didn't see anything wrong with that. She reasoned it as "they weren't meant to be", but I secretly thought she was messed up. Girls that did stuff like that were the ones I wanted to beat up in high school.

"There's no reason to be friends with him on Facebook. I wouldn't want random people requesting my husband. But seriously, why would anyone want to get married so young? What a waste. He probably hasn't even like, lived yet," I complained.

I was done with the idea and that was it. I wanted nothing to do with a married guy, let alone a married couple. I had no business being around married people anyway, I was in the prime years of my life: my twenties. I was young, wild, and free. I was still bothered but I brushed it off, fighting the urge to think about him.

That weekend, I went to a concert with Christina and Blake. Jax was there with Ben and a few mutual friends. The venue was packed. During the opening band, the girls and I kept to ourselves in the corner until we decided it was time to take some shots. We sat at the bar and ordered a round as Jax walked by and ordered a beer. Noticing me, he said hello and referenced a conversation we had the night we had met.

Jax was much more talkative this time and we got into a debate about a new album that had just been released. It took a few moments until I realized that he was staring at me as hard as I was staring at him. Time halted. All of a sudden, it was as if the entire world melted away and it was just, us, in that venue talking alone.

We spent a good while there before his wife tapped him

on his shoulder and pulled him away as the lights went low in anticipation for the headlining band. I felt her stare and realizing the awkwardness, became embarrassed that I had been talking so long to somebody that was married. I figured Jax was just being friendly, after all, I was a guy's girl. I was easy to talk to.

I turned to my friends. They were staring at me with their mouths open, eyes wide. "What?!" I asked.

They looked around. "He LIKES you," Blake whistled. Christina nodded.

"What are you talking about? I met him the other night at Harley's, we were just talking about music," I responded, my cheeks turning red.

"That dude, like, loves you. You can tell. The way he looked at you in your eyes? You don't stare at someone like that unless you're interested," Blake continued to go on as I finished my drink in complete dismay.

"He's married to her," I tilted my head towards his wife, who was now sizing me up a few feet away, whispering with her friends.

"That's the guy you were telling me about?" Christina asked. I nodded.

"Oh." Blake replied, confused. "I thought he was single. How was I supposed to know? They don't look like they're together, let alone married." She sipped her drink and changed the subject. The headlining band started their set and I dazed out, confused.

What the hell happened? I had literally lost myself in talking to him. That had never happened before. I had a weird feeling in my gut. 'This is The One' my brain kept saying but I tried to shut it off. How could Jax be The One if he was already somebody else's One? Why had we been making such intense eye contact? There was no way in the world I could have feelings for a married guy! I wasn't "that girl" and I refused to be "that girl".

Blake was right though, those two were basically avoiding each other. Jax was hanging out by himself watching the band alone, as she ignored him, laughing and hanging out with her friends. I shook my head and forced the thought of it all out of my brain. Their relationship wasn't my business. This was all ridiculous and stupid to even consider.

A few days later, Ben told me to come check out his new apartment. I was bartending that night so I promised I would pop in before I went. That afternoon, I had to run errands and got home later than I anticipated, so I got dressed and rushed to Ben's apartment because I would only be able to stay for a few minutes before I had to go to Harley's. I knocked on the door and Ben answered. I marveled at how cute his apartment was and then I noticed Jax sitting there on the couch watching TV with a beer in hand.

My heart dropped and I was caught off guard but I didn't skip a beat, apologizing that I would only be able to stay for a couple of minutes. I engaged in conversation, noticing Jax's eyes on me the whole time, but I tried to avoid him, not making eye contact. The truth was, he was so friendly that it was hard not to be drawn to him.

Eventually I left, content with the fact that Jax would be another good guy friend to have. He seemed like a great person with good intentions and I resolved to myself that we could be friends. Since we were hanging out with mutual friends more and more, like Ben, I figured this was just a new person to get to know. He was cute but he was married, and that was the end of it for me. I imagined him living happily ever after with his life and so I tried to continue on with my mine, ignoring the aching feeling that I had met the right guy at the wrong time.

*

Jax wasn't living happily ever after, by any means: he regretted his decision on getting married so young. He came from a great family, loving parents and siblings he adored, and he wanted that – he wanted to be the family man that his father was. Unfortunately, a few weeks after his wedding, it became clear to him that the person he had married was not the person he wanted to spend the rest of his life with.

He tried to look past his constant dread of waking up each morning next to the wrong person but it got harder and harder. He didn't want to admit that he had made a mistake getting married so young because he knew what people would say: well then, why did you? Even worse, he understood that reaction because he wondered himself, why had he?

Jax, desperately seeking someone that he could confide in and let 'it all out' to, started coming to the bar. He had enjoyed our previous conversations and sensed that I was a good person to get advice from because the combination of being a writer and a bartender indicated that I had a way with words. Being an introvert, Jax had pushed his voice down for too long and he appreciated that I valued what he had to say.

He poured his heart out about his conflicted unhappiness and his fear of disappointing the people he loved the most…his parents. He would gaze into my eyes and look away, hurt. It was heart wrenching to hear, not only because I knew Jax was so unhappy, but also because I wanted him to be happy…with me.

Realizing I had feelings for Jax made me no longer recognize myself – who was I? I was playing with fire, but still, I reasoned there was nothing wrong with becoming friends with Jax because all we were doing was talking…even if it was a lot. Then, a lot more. No boundaries were crossed - but we became each other's confidants. We found a kind of rapport in one another that we had never found before with anyone else. Fighting himself, he had resolved to try to work it out, but time was up: he couldn't do it anymore. It was time to ask for a divorce.

That night, Jax asked to meet up with me. He paced back and forth telling me that he was in agony, stifling thoughts of suicide. He didn't know what was worse, spending the rest of his life with the wrong person or ending his life. He was despondent but determined to get a divorce.

"You can't get divorced! Think of what people would say," I said.

"Nobody has to live my life but me and I can't live like this anymore," he said, distraught.

"Yeah, but still…." I didn't know how to advise him in an unbiased way at this point.

"I feel like I met the right person at the worst possible time," he said, looking at me, beginning to cry as he covered his face in his hands. I knew what he meant. A flood of emotions crept up on me as I realized this was really happening, that this was real. We had feelings for each other.

I let it all out to Jax: that I had known he was special from the day I met him, and that ever since, I had been fighting feelings for him. He admitted that on top of not wanting to be married anymore, he had been fighting feelings for me too. As a result, he was torn between suffering in his marriage for 'appearances sake' and actually being happy. It would be wrong to stay married just to make everybody else satisfied. Besides that, he couldn't. He just couldn't.

"Why would God make us meet if he knew we couldn't be together?" he cried. I froze as he echoed the thoughts I had been thinking silently to myself ever since I met him.

I sat in silence, pondering the same thing, when it occurred to me, "Maybe God made us meet so we COULD be together." We started at each other with hope because we knew deep down, that was exactly why.

There was a heaviness in the room – we knew we were in a situation that would be almost impossible to escape from, unscarred – but there was also an electric excitement exuding from the both of us. Something was guiding us to be together and now acknowledging that we both felt it, we decided that it was time to make it happen. So we set off to do just that – and found a little piece of Heaven in Hell on Earth.

Point Me At Lost Islands

Jax asked for a divorce. Rumors were created and stories were twisted, with not an inkling of truth to any of them, but they spread like wildfire across Meadows regardless. I didn't even have the opportunity to defend myself but honestly, nobody would have cared anyway. When people were told that Jax had asked for a divorce 'because he had met me', people automatically considered me the villain. "You could have anyone you want, why'd you have to pick a married guy?" they accused, as if things were that simple. It didn't help that I had made tons of enemies during my Sam and Dylan years that there were people just aching to exchange horror stories about me. I was the Meadows home-wrecker, shamefully carrying around a Scarlett letter, and painfully aware of the looks full of disgust that were thrown my way.

Unfortunately, not only were these looks coming from

strangers, but they were also coming from people I had loved my whole life. I could deal with being publicly trashed on social media by people who didn't know me, although that hurt a lot. I could deal with the nasty looks, the edging away from me as if I was contagious, but that too, secretly hurt me down to my core. I could deal with people who didn't know me trashing my name – but what devastated me the most was losing people who DID know me.

Sasha decided she didn't want to be associated with me. She expected more from me and promptly dropped me as a friend. She had been 'raised better than that', alluding to the fact that I was raised not to be. The gossip was such a minor part of a much bigger person – and instead of loving me, she judged me too. This was a person who knew that deep down, I was a good person. If I hadn't been, why did she share her life with me all those years? She didn't even ask to hear my side of the story, she simply unfriended me on Facebook and then in real life too.

Christina and Blake followed suit shortly after, not wanting to be seen in public with Meadows Most Hated. Almost immediately, the three girls I had been loyal to my whole life discarded me as if I was trash. This resulted in friendship break-ups that would make all of the ones I went through look like child's play because this time, it was forever. They dropped me when I needed them the most and I knew there was no going back to those fraudulent friendships. Losing them as friends was like experiencing a death – the death of those friendships, the death of my old life, the death of the old me. Adjusting to life without them was harsh, but in the end, I needed to.

I had spent my life trying to not become a statistic, trying to be a good person, and I had ruined my reputation for a man. Deep down, my brain and my heart kept insisting that Jax was going to be the one who made all of this chaos worth it. In a few years, we would laugh about all of this when it was our turn to live happily ever. It would be worth it - we both knew it – and so, I followed my heart.

It was the smartest thing I've ever done.

*

At the end of the day, my name would now represent every woman's worst fear: someone in better shape, someone with a 'better' look, someone stealing the person you love, even if that wasn't at all the real situation behind closed doors. It didn't matter that Jax and his ex had much bigger problems; once I entered the picture, I took the burden of the blame. I became the scapegoat, but the truth is…a marriage is between two people…and I wasn't one of them.

Our love story would forever be tainted as two people who met, fell in love, but 'shouldn't have'. The entire situation also guaranteed that whenever his ex would do something in her life or I would do something in mine, people would be running to each side to fill each other in. My daily doings were no longer mine anymore, they became gossip at dinner tables and bars. I was now a 'celebrity' in my hometown, but it wasn't for the right reasons. I would go through the rest of my life in

Meadows known as a home-wrecker.

It was more than I could bear but I had no choice. When you're down that far in a hole, your only options are self-destructing or carrying on. I chose to carry on, walking over broken pieces of my fully in love heart shattered at my feet.

*

Jax quickly found a studio apartment near his job. Even though his new place was a downgrade from what he was used to, he tried to make it as welcoming as possible. It was difficult, considering the apartment was old, dusty, and smelled like mothballs. The shower pipes were so old that he had to take showers wearing sandals, because the water would fill up in the tub and the floor felt gross underneath his feet. The walls were made up of wood paneling and the kitchen wallpaper was retro brown with orange flowers, something you'd expect to see in your grandmother's home. He had to take hand me downs from his relatives so he had furniture. He didn't care though, and neither did I - we were just happy that we could now spend time together now that the divorce was finalized.

The beginning of our relationship was nothing short of less than ideal. We got to know each other fairly quick as we hid out in his apartment, afraid to run into anybody from Meadows by venturing out. Our hearts couldn't take the dirty looks and whispers anymore so we stayed in most nights, talking and bonding. I told him things I've never told anybody else.

On our first real date, Jax took me roller-skating. We figured we wouldn't run into anybody from Meadows but since it was the only roller rink around, we knew that if we did run into somebody we knew, we would just have to deal with it. We enjoyed our first real date, roller-skating and holding hands while listening to 80's music.

When we were done, I went to exchange the skates I had rented for my shoes. I waited on line and heard somebody cough behind me. I turned around and noticed a girl from Meadows, who was also known as the town gossip, standing behind me. As she noticed me look at her, she made a disapproving face and grabbed her phone to text. My head began to fill up with thoughts of wondering who she was texting, what she was relaying, and why she was writing whatever she was writing. Jax and I left a few minutes later and I had a full-blown panic attack once we got in the car.

It was the first of many. I went from being mentally strong to very weak. I developed severe, crippling anxiety every time I had to leave the house so I found reasons not to. I had always been anxious, but at this point, the walls came crashing down. Days were spent with my lungs constantly restricted, my chest tight, migraines pounding into my head as my blood twinkled brutally from the inside. It's hard to explain but my whole body felt as heavy as the Earth. It was anxiety - stemmed from fear, hurt, and hopelessness.

The fall out from the Jax saga was unrelenting and everyday I felt the repercussions from us being together. Most people were appalled at how quickly we started dating, but what they didn't realize was that we really didn't have a choice.

When it feels like the entire world is against you, it makes you connect even deeper to the one that you know isn't. At that point, all we had was each other and in the end, this served to make our bond even stronger.

Regardless of the strength of our connection, I was still bordering on the edge of a type of anxiety I had never known before, the kind that consumes you, that you drown in. I had absolutely no idea what to do with myself. I would cry for hours out of nowhere. This is the part of my story where I break apart for good, pain streaming out of me like a river, tears embedded in my pores. I become vulnerable.

My life as I knew it was officially different – and I didn't want it to be. Why couldn't I have my old life, but with Jax in it? I was riddled with sadness. I was embarrassed, ashamed, depressed, and angry. Jax held me as I sobbed, throwing things and screaming. I had lost so much already, would I ever be fully happy again? Not just 'relationship-happy', but life-happy? Most importantly, self-happy?

I would cry so much and shake so hard that Jax would have to spend hours rubbing my back and stroking my hair with hopes that I would calm down. I would, but only by the time I fell asleep. My doctor recommended taking anti anxiety medicine, but I quickly told him I would get through this on my own... even if it killed me.

Jax and I hadn't been together for long by the time he had to endure the brutal task of taking care of me during one of these hysterical episodes – but he did it. He was the only one who could. He watched me crack apart at my darkest moments and still loved me. It took time but I eventually let him save me from myself. Somehow, Jax loved me back to life.

*

One night, after watching a show that included a young couple with a toddler, I looked over to Jax and for the first time ever, had a shooting image in my head of me with a baby. What shocked me even further was that Jax was next to me, as the father. I smiled to myself. He noticed. "Why are you smiling?"

"Do you want to have children?" I asked, curious. We were still getting to know each other, even if we were moving at a fast pace. I wasn't embarrassed to ask and it was probably something I needed to know if I planned on spending the rest of my life with him.

The look in his eyes as he answered made my stomach feel like butterflies were being released into the wild. "Yes, with the right person." He smiled, grabbing my entire body into a tight bear hug, kissing me. I felt electric chills down my back as I realized, this was the man who I would marry and (hopefully) create a family with.

Jax was my soulmate, now my partner through life, and that made beginning to move on with my life that much more important. I started seeking out ways to do it, for good this time.

*

I wanted to escape New Jersey for a week and Jax

happily agreed to come to California, so we quickly booked our flight, our hotel room, and rented a convertible. A week later we were in the air, looking out the window, anxious to leave it all behind.

This particular trip was a big one in terms of my relationship with Jax because I had never been on vacation with a boyfriend before. I knew if I couldn't have fun with him in Hollywood, then he wouldn't be someone I could marry. I decided that that would be my 'test' for men from now on.

I wouldn't need to cash in on any more chances – Jax turned out to be the perfect companion.

*

DJ grilled Jax as soon as he opened our hotel room door. He was intrigued to meet the guy who had scored me, a little-sister type, who had been the sullen 'hard to get' bartender back in Jersey. Within minutes, DJ was hugging Jax and patting me on the back saying, "I like this guy! Good job." I immediately fell in love with DJ's new girlfriend Nancy, a spunky San Diego chick who had fire engine red hair and a smile that made you smile too. The four of us hit it off and set off to the Rainbow to get dinner, where our other friends were waiting for us.

Jax met the rest of the Cali crew. Now this is where it could have gotten tricky, but I didn't have to be concerned – everyone loved him. Thankfully, Jax was musically inclined, so he found himself drifting off into conversations with some friends who were musicians, while I caught up with Diane.

"He's great," Diane whispered to me. I smiled to myself. She was right, he really was.

It was thrilling to see him in his element, next to me in mine, and I realized this was the first time we were able to be ourselves, out in the open, without having to look around us. To my friends in California, Jax and I weren't the villains in a hometown scandal, we were a normal couple, so we were able to breathe with ease. I felt the release of a burden on my shoulders as I ran over to Jax and hugged him, openly kissing the man I cared about. We opened up, being affectionate and adoring, and our relationship fully blossomed that night in Los Angeles. There, we could just be us. Around people. In public. Enjoying the night. Just living our lives.

The rest of the week was nothing short of a dream: we took walks on the beach, posing for pictures at sunset, and took a short trip to San Diego. We parked on Mulholland at nighttime and watched the city twinkle beneath our feet as we held each other and told each other "I love you" for the first time. We got dressed up to the nines and went to Hyde, having a great boyfriend/girlfriend kind of night that included dancing, drinking, and lots of groping. We were drunk in love with the feeling of being our authentic selves in Los Angeles.

It was on that trip that I found myself experiencing something I had never done before: making love. The kind of making love where you feel your body melt into the other person's, where you feel electricity transferring from your soul onto theirs. With other guys, I had sex, but with Jax...we made love. I knew I could never sleep with anybody else again and better yet, I knew I would never want to. This trip solidified to me that I had been right to follow my heart because our relationship was on a different level – our love was the real deal.

This Charming Life

Knowing in my heart that Jax was The One, we decided to move in together, in order to start the beginning of our life together for real. Being in Los Angeles and being able to be open and loving to each other reminded us that we deserved to be happy too. We had suffered enough and it was time to finally be ourselves. We eventually found a place together a few towns away from Meadows.

I relished in 'playing house' with Jax. I liked cleaning the floors and going food shopping together, picking out things to make for dinner. I loved picking out furniture. I enjoyed trying to organize the kitchen and the bedroom to make it look somewhat like a home for us. I marveled at my own growth as a homemaker and found myself wanting to spend more money at Bed, Bath, and Beyond than at Sephora. Nobody was more surprised than me when I started turning down parties to watch Netflix with Jax at home – but it was happening: I was becoming domesticated.

I was officially in an adult relationship… that wasn't always perfect. We disagreed over what to eat and what to watch on TV. I sighed when he didn't pick up his clothes as he made faces scooping my hair out of the shower drain. We bickered about all the things that couples that live together bicker about… and we couldn't have been happier.

Life was going on and we were going with it.

*

Time passed and things started to settle down. Jax and I began to enjoy our life together, publicly. We were doing it with a lot less "friends", but my real friends, including The Guys and Katie, stuck around and welcomed Jax with open arms. We started to show face at various functions and tried to infiltrate ourselves back in mainstream society being proud of who we were and what we were to each other. Things became 'normal' and routine, something most girls find boring, but I couldn't have been more thankful for.

Jax and I were as adoring of each other in public as we were privately. Once naysayers saw the obvious vibe between us, they softened on their opinions, which made living our lives a little bit easier. It was a relief – people were starting to understand that Jax and I weren't a 'fling' and surprisingly, we complemented each other in wonderful ways. I brought him out of his shell and he mellowed me out.

The undeniable truth was that Jax and I ended up

together because we had to be together; there was no other way. Luckily for us, after seeing us together, nobody could deny that. Even if they tried to, it wouldn't matter. Our connection spoke for itself.

*

I was still suffering from mourning the loss of some of my friendships, but I just had to accept it. I found the love of my life, but he came with a price. You know how most stories have endings that readers are at peace with? My friendships with Sasha, Christina, and Blake don't. I followed my heart and they followed the crowd.

Life goes on and I had no choice but to continue growing as a person without them by my side. My entire life, I had always had the girls to rely on, but now that I knew they could turn on me the one time I needed them the most, there was no reason to romanticize such toxic friendships. I eventually realized this loss was a blessing. The painful truth of it all was that at the end of the day, I had always loved them more than they loved me. I decided to privately and quietly love them from a distance.

The most painful thing about losing Sasha, Christina, and Blake was that we grew together, we learned together, we evolved together - our lives were truly intertwined. We contributed to the women we are today... and now, we'll never know how the other turned out.

*

Many times, I ended up sitting home alone, lost in my thoughts. One afternoon, I glanced over to my laptop on my bedside table. I opened it and stared at it. I hadn't really written much in terms of diary-like entries since my last journal had been stolen by Sam's ex Rebecca back in high school, but that day something in me told me it was time to start writing again. Besides, I needed an outlet where I could get all of my emotions out of my system. I took a deep breath... and then, my fingers started to move, prompting me to write. I let my emotions pour out as I pounded on the keys, crying all over them. Once I started, I couldn't stop.

Writing became my way of healing and I threw myself into it as much as I could. It was better therapy than anything I could have ever paid for. I took the heartache and made it work in my favor by creating my own version of art. That Toshiba laptop provided a basis for daily artistic therapy, with Microsoft Word providing the canvas and the letter keys becoming my paint. I began to spend all of my days writing, eventually finding a friend in my laptop. I wrote angry poetry, as well as letters that would never be sent. I found myself being surprised, reading thoughts that I didn't even know I had. I set off to cure myself. I started writing all of the hurt out.

*

Life fully balanced itself out. My mother made great progress after seeking therapy and was now leading a much happier life. Jax and I were eventually replaced by various new town scandals and we started a wholesome life together. Now a college graduate, I took on a few different jobs, like being a Pre-K teacher, only to find out that my heart truly longed to be in the writing industry. I had always dreamed of being an established writer – and now, I was going to try.

I began to gain my confidence and self esteem back up. I also began yoga and meditation, which truly helped my anxiety. Meditation brought upon a new scale of awareness that I had never known before, and I found myself becoming more in tune with myself. Now understanding the power of prayer, I also began to pray for those I loved...and those I lost.

A person's true character is displayed during the darkest of times. Finally understanding that losing people I had thought loved me should make me appreciate the ones who actually did, I began to spend more and more time with family and our friends who had stuck by us. I began to love them in a different, elevated way than I had before.

I was changing as a person. After everything I had been through, I had been humbled as a human being. I now had an even stronger sense of empathy and I wasn't apologetic for it. Instead of using my strength as a defense mechanism, I became more compassionate and softer; listening instead of speaking, understanding and not judging, and routinely putting myself in other people's shoes. I became truly dedicated to becoming a better person and I did. It was then that I realized everything in my life had truly happened for a reason.

*

That year of my life was literally the most challenging. Between my mother's depression, graduating college, being involved in a town scandal, losing friends, having to decide on my future and finding Jax – I was initially lost.

Lost, lost, lost.

Throughout that time of drowning in my own sea of tears, being on my own, sitting in silence, dealing with my new reality and learning how to cope through it to survive it, that year turned out to be the best year of my life because not only had I found myself through my writing, but I had also found the world's kindest, most genuine, loving man.

A man who would show me layers of real love that I had never known before. A man who had chosen to go through hell and back just to be with ME. A man who would be my soulmate in every sense of the word.

I knew Jax was the person my father had pointed out to God and said, "That's the man I want for my daughter."

For the first time ever, *I considered myself lucky.*

*

Four years later, I went back to California with Jax. The moment we arrived, Jax eagerly insisted on driving to the Hollywood sign. I was hesitant because I wanted to meet up with our friends that we hadn't seen in a while. I suggested that we go see it the next day when we were settled but he insisted, so we sat in traffic during sundown on our way through the Hollywood Hills to the sign. The traffic annoyed me so I complained about us hurrying up once we got there, not knowing Jax had a surprise waiting for me. We drove through the hills to our favorite spot and once we parked, I rushed up the canyon with Jax slowly trailing behind me.

As soon as I got to the top, I was surprised to see hundreds of lit tea candles on the ground, illuminating as the Hollywood Sign floated over us. As I got closer, I realized the candles were positioned to spell out something and I gasped when I read the words:

WILL YOU MARRY ME?

I turned around to Jax to see him on one knee, holding a tiny maroon ring box. He stared into my eyes and smiled. "I love you so much, Ellie. I want to spend the rest of my life with you. Will you marry me?" he asked.

Shaking, I said yes and we hugged each other, crying tears of joy. DJ and Nancy, responsible for setting up the candles, popped out from behind the mountain and congratulated us. It was the most amazing moment of my life – even better than I had ever dreamed of as a child. It was the first time I had ever cried happy tears.

That trip to California was full of excitement, shared happiness, and lots of making love. I was finally getting the happy ending that I had once dreamt about. It was the best couple of days of my life.

Only If For A Night

Until Friday morning, when I woke up.

In my dreams, it's his turn to shine. He is royally dressed, not wearing white like you would expect angels to wear, but bright red and yellow, like his favorite sweatshirt. As my brain shuffles the dream around in my head as I sleep, I am always surprised to see him pop up out of nowhere. He comes at the right time, just as the climax of the dream is getting to the point where I am now, literally, sweating in my sleep.

In this dream, I am back in high school. The school looks the same, lockers in the same spot. As I rifle through my old locker, I notice that I have left something in there, from years ago. I am surprised to see a note from him. I remember his handwriting. Things get tense. I become upset. I notice that things seem the same, as though I was still in high school, but things aren't the same because now, he's gone.

Suddenly, he appears, all in bright colors. He is young again, with the same fresh face that I had grown to love. He is skinny and his hair is short and shaved on the side. He glides toward me as if he were walking on clouds, yet I am walking on eggshells. He stops in front of me and looks deep into my eyes.

In my dreams, he is truly there. If the afterlife is real, instead of wandering around the earth invisible, he has planted himself in my dreams so I can meet him at night when I sleep.

I can touch him, so I reach out and press my hand against his face. He smiles. I smile. He stares so intensely that I begin to get overwhelmed. I begin to say "I wish you were real" but he stops me, grabs me gently, and holds me as we float down the halls, my head resting on his shoulder.

He holds me up the entire time.

*

In another dream, we are in a beautiful palace. It is made out of burgundy marble, and inside, the entire place consists of libraries. The room I first see him in has a two level library full of books that are just begging to be read. He appears. He is sitting on a beautifully constructed wooden chair that looks almost like a throne...but the man I know wouldn't be so narcissistic. I can't reach him. I grow frustrated that he is just sitting there, reading a book, instead of acknowledging my presence.

Just like the old days.

At one point, I engage in such rage that he has no point but to notice me. He gets up, glides towards me again, and sets himself in front of me. I can see his face as though it were real. "Prove it!" I scream, "Prove that you are real!" He nods with sympathetic eyes, understanding, and begins to take his t-shirt off. I laugh, amused by the image of him shimmying his shirt off like a Calvin Klein model. His torso still looks the same.

Still, I am not convinced. I shake my head, insisting on more proof. He points to his tattoos, some of which I always thought were ridiculous, but I have come to appreciate more so now. I remember them well. Still not good enough. "No," I begin, "It's not enough-."

Suddenly he grabs my face and kisses my mouth. His

taste is familiar – its nostalgia. It's Winterfresh. Like the first kiss I ever had. I realize and I turn away, because this is not real. I am now engaged to the love of my life…and it is not him.

I wake up.

Freebird

That Friday morning, I wake up happily hung over to an overwhelming amount of text messages. I groaned, not wanting to know what kind of drama I was missing back home, but I opened my inbox anyway.

My heart stopped for a whole minute as I read the texts, telling me that Sam was dead. The universe, time, and reality paused in that moment. Each text message said the same thing: Sam was gone. He had been killed in a car accident with a drunk driver while sitting in the middle of the backseat of a friend's car. He hadn't been wearing a seat belt and when the drunk driver collided with the rear end of the car, the impact of the crash forced Sam through the windshield. He was pronounced dead on the scene, but according to the people who were with him, they watched him take his last breath way before ambulances got there to declare the time of death.

Immediately, I was inconsolable. I couldn't believe it. I

began calling people back home. My friends were disappointed I had found out because they wanted to wait until I got home to tell me - they didn't want my engagement to be affected. Other people from Meadows, well, they tripped over themselves to be the ones to break the news.

All I cared about was that somebody who had been so significant in my life was now gone, for good. And here I was, partying like it was the end of the world and enjoying my engagement. I felt guilty and ungrateful, like I had no right to be happy when Sam had lost his life the day before.

Even though I had found myself disconnected from my grandfather's death, I was deeply affected by Sam's. As a kid, you grow up knowing that your grandparents will probably pass away at some point because they are older and that's how life works. But Sam was only a few years older than me and he had a whole life ahead of him, just like I did. The mere idea of him missing out on the rest of his life was hard to come to terms with. It wasn't fair.

After all, this was the first person who had paved the way for all the other guys in my life... he was the one who educated me on what I deserved out of a relationship. The lessons I learned when I was with him, when I wasn't with him, and when we were good friends...I will forever be indebted to him.

For the rest of my vacation, I tried to enjoy myself. It's hard not to, when you have California inviting you to enjoy its beauty...but I found myself having to force a smile at times. Poor Jax, he had planned this remarkable proposal only for it to be affected by the death of my ex a few days later. It was important to me that I didn't let Sam's death impact our engagement, so I put on a happy face for Jax, but Sam was a constant in my thoughts. I found myself drifting into deep thought of old memories. I thought about the time he showed up to my house with that registered star in my name. I thought about the way he looked at me with his eyes that had put me in a crazy frenzy for so many years. For the first time ever, all I could think about were the good times...I literally forgot about all of the bad.

The day we were leaving to go back home, I insisted on stopping at Sunset Live! so I could pick up a headband that I had seen a couple of days before. I knew I would never spend fifty dollars on a headband back at home and since I had some cash left in my 'vacation fund', I figured I would treat myself one last time. Jax parked the car and I ran across the street. I walked up to the Sunset Live! door, only to see that the store was closed on Sundays. Bummed, I began my way back to the car.

As I stopped at the corner, there was a girl standing next to me, talking on her cell phone. She had a lovely British accent, and for some reason, I was drawn to it. The light changed, and we began to walk across the street, with me walking behind her in a daze. We got to the corner and because I was too busy listening to her, I forgot where I was for a second and began to walk across the next street towards our rental car.

The girl stopped, but I kept going, lost in my own world, as a white truck came zooming towards me because it was a green light. The girl screamed at me to move as the truck came right at me and I froze - not having enough time for my brain to formulate the idea of getting out of the way - when an invisible cold force pushed me to the side, hard and strong, with so much urgency I fell.

"Are you okay? That was the bloody craziest thing I've ever seen," the British girl said in shock, running over to me to help me pick myself up off the ground. All I could do was nod, gather myself, and continue my walk to the car as soon as the pedestrian light popped up.

When I hopped in the car, I began to sob so heavily that it came from my stomach. Jax wanted to know what happened but it was hard to explain…and even harder to understand. I knew that something had pushed me out of harms way… but what could it have been? Had it been Sam? I had always heard stories about guardian angels… but I had also heard about aliens and the Loch Ness Monster. Things that you always hear about…but are most likely untrue. If anyone were my guardian angel, wouldn't it have been my father? In fact, don't people get appointed guardian angels when they are born?

Suddenly, it dawned on me that this vacation had been anything but. In seven days, I was proposed to, became engaged to the love of my life, lost my first love, and had a supernatural experience that my fiancée just nodded along to, as if he was amusing me by pretending to believe me.

I thought about it the entire red-eye plane ride home. The fact that I wasn't paying attention while crossing the street was one thing, but something cold and strong pushing me out of the way when the truck zoomed towards me was another. As Jax slept, I was restless, unable to read any of the books I had brought for the flight. I looked ahead of me at the seat pocket and my eyes fixated on the headline of the first magazine in sight, ahead of the complimentary Sky Mall.

"Los Angeles," the cover read, "The City of Angels."

*

The next day back at home was a whirlwind. We came home to family and friends who were excited that we were now engaged, but I had to spend my night after a long jet-lagged day back at work looking for pictures of Sam to display at his wake. There were so many: pictures of him at football games and pictures of him at my birthday party holding up my birthday cake. Pictures of him making the peace sign in his first car and pictures of him sleeping peacefully.

Out of all those pictures, there was only one of him and I together, from my freshman year in high school. It was taken at a friend's sweet sixteen and we are sitting at a table with Maggie and Jordan. He is wearing a Hawaiian shirt and his head is shaved. I am across from him, wearing a faux leather jacket.

The thing that stands out about this picture is that we both have huge grins on our faces and we are looking right at each other. Sam made a joke and I laughed, and the camera just happened to catch that moment at the right time. I hate the way I look when I laugh, and I usually cover my mouth because I dislike my teeth, but in this picture I am oblivious to how I look and you can see the joy on my young face. My eyes are semi-closed, but his are wide. It is a beautiful moment captured.

Maybe I'm biased but when I look at the picture, I can see the love. I can feel myself in that moment, back to that day. It was a Sunday after we had spent the prior Friday and Saturday driving around town, making out, and we had finally gone to 'second base'. I was embarrassed to see him the next day. I blushed the entire time and was unusually quiet but Sam, sensing my uneasiness, made me feel comfortable. He made silly jokes and flirted with me to ease the awkwardness that he had just gone up my shirt the night before. When I look at that picture, I see young love at its most innocent. I see young me.

I chose to go to Sam's wake alone, so I was relieved to arrive at the funeral home and see Maggie and Molly waiting for me at the door. I hadn't seen Molly since we had graduated high school and as soon as she caught sight of me, she grabbed me and hugged me so tight I thought my rib cage was going to crack. We chained our arms together along with Maggie and walked into Sam's wake together in somber silence.

His wake was awful. There is no other way to put it. I don't know any other person who has heard, "I'm so sorry to hear about Sam! I know how much you loved him when you were younger. Oh, and by the way, congratulations on your engagement!" as soon as they walk into a wake. It was devastating. The only thing that made it bearable was his family, especially his lovely mother, who told me to "shine on" for Sam. I promised her I would. I meant it.

For days, I agonized over the whole situation. The last

time I saw Sam alive, I was driving in Jax's car and he was in his car and we drove past each other. We locked eyes and waved. I thought about him that day. What was he up to now? Had he found a girlfriend, the kind his mother would love? The last time we had hung out, he was in good spirits, keeping me company during my day shift at Harley's. We talked for a while, him joking that I should "dump the hero and get with the zero" and us laughing in comfortable unison.

Being around Sam was good for the soul. I knew he regretted the way things had happened with us because he realized that if he had just treated me right, maybe I would have stayed with him and we could have been happy. That's not the way our story turned out. I changed, he changed, and life changed us. We grew up.

A week after the wake, I allowed myself to start getting excited about planning my wedding. I spent tons of money on wedding magazines and started considering themes. Jax and I started looking at venues for our engagement party and discussed our budget. I consumed myself with wedding dresses and kept busy.

The almost-getting-hit-by-a-truck-in-LA thing was still weighing heavily on my mind. I needed closure...better yet, I needed answers. I needed to know whether or not Sam had been the one to push me out of the way.

On my way home from work I decided it was time to ask for a sign and I looked around for an idea on what to ask for. I silently asked God/the universe/the powers that be to show me the number 27 (Sam's favorite number and high school beeper code) if he had been the one to push me out of the way of that truck.

Within the thirty seconds it took me to finish asking for the silent request of showing me the number 27, I passed a brand new sign showing the way towards Route 27 in big, bold black letters. I drove the same route to and from work every single day, yet there it was, a brand new sign right on the corner, freshly installed. A bird was perched on the sign, looking at me.

Suddenly my radio, the same one that hadn't worked in years, forcing me to listen to nothing but CDs, was no longer broken – a static-y song began to blast through my speakers.

It was "Freebird".

I ripped off my sunglasses with my mouth dropping open as tears welled up. I looked down and the radio was on q104.3, the red numbers bright and bold. My skin turned cold and goose bumps climbed up my arms. I froze, blocking out the people honking around me, and listened closely.

As the song went on, I thought back to that night, our first time talking on the phone, when Sam told me to turn on the radio because "Freebird" was playing. *"He's telling someone he loves that he has to go explore other worlds. He's got to fly away and be a free bird."* At that exact moment, the bird flew away.

My question had been answered: Sam had saved my life that day. I knew in that moment that wherever he was, he was a free bird. He couldn't be there for me in the flesh, but he was going to be there for me in spirit. Our souls would meet again.

I drove off, smiling to myself at my newfound peace, enjoying the music as the strong summer sunrays shifted into my point of view. Basking in the warmth of their light, I didn't bother putting my sunglasses back on...

I just let them shine.

Come To Me
(Epilogue)

On May 12th, I married Jax, the love of my life, in front of all of our friends, family, and God. I found myself breathing a breath of relief when I woke up that morning and realized that the overwhelming stress I found from wedding planning would be over by the end of the night. As a bonus, I would also be married to my favorite person on this Earth.

That morning, I woke up and fought nerve-wracking anxiety and instantly, ran to the window to see how the weather was. After a harsh winter, spring had brought nothing but rain every single day the past few weeks, so I was literally praying for good weather. To my delighted surprise, it was a beautiful day. The sun was shining and the weather topped out at 75 degrees, a true relief from the brutal weather New Jersey-ians had endured that winter. It was the first nice day of the year – and it just so happened to be my wedding day. I stared at the sky and smiled to myself. Somebody had heard my prayers and once again, answered them.

The rest of the day was a whirlwind of events. I got dressed with my bridesmaids, did yoga to calm my nerves, and I ate toast and drank apple juice in an attempt to not throw up out of nervousness. My hair and makeup were done and now there was nothing left to do but to walk down the aisle to my fiancée and declare my undying love for him in front of everyone we knew. Easy!

When it was time, my mother and I stopped at the beginning of the aisle and we smiled, hugging each other. "I wish your father could see you in this moment," my mother said, against my cheek.

"I know," I said, holding back tears.

With that being said, my mother squeezed my hand and began to walk me down the aisle, clutching my arm and crying. I knew she was crying tears of happiness because I was marrying a great man, but I knew some of those tears stemmed from the fact that it was her walking me down the aisle, and not my father. For another flashing second, I thought to myself how I wished my father could be there with us in that moment. I brushed it off.

The ceremony was beautiful and the reception was a blast. We enjoyed our wedding day, complete with personal touches of our personalities throughout. It was a day far more beautiful than anything I could put into words but the love exuded off of everybody with us. Jax and I were beginning the rest of our lives together, just like we were meant to. We had our happy ending, or rather, our happy new beginning.

The next day, I had an email from our photographer

who was thanking us for letting him be a part of our day. Attached in the email was the first professional picture from our wedding that he had uploaded: a picture of Jax and I, posing in front of an elegant water fountain outside the venue against trees and a little river, complete with a colorful rainbow. I was breathless once I saw the happy glow on our faces.

"Look babe!" I said excitedly, showing him the picture. He smirked, kissing me on the head, and laid his head on my chest. I stared at the picture, basking in the beauty of that image, when I noticed something strange.

"What is that?" I asked, staring closer.

"What?" Jax asked, looking at me. Noticing a look on my face that he had never seen before, he stared into the picture too. His jaw dropped as he realized what I was fixated on.

We studied closely, neither of us saying anything until we were confident that our eyes weren't playing tricks on us. It seemed impossible, but within the beams of the sun, was in fact, was my father's face shining through the rainbow. His dark hair, the shape of his face, his eyes and beard – it was there, in faint sight. Turned to the left slightly, it was almost as though he was looking down on us…just like all those times I had stared up at the sky and wished he had been.

"It's my father," I whispered softly, hoping that by saying those mere words it wouldn't make him go away. As I felt the hot heat of tears fill up my face, I sat there stunned, not fighting them back. I let them roll.

Almost immediately, I emailed our photographer back, asking if he had noticed my father's face in the rainbow.

"Wow," he wrote, *"No, I didn't. I've never seen anything like that. It looks like your father was with you on your wedding day! What a miracle!"*

I couldn't believe it, but it was real. My father's face in my wedding photo, proving that he had been there on my wedding day, was real. All those times I had prayed and spoken to him, he had been listening. Heaven, angels, and the afterlife – it was all real. My spirit soared to new heights knowing this.

A montage of memories started to flood my thoughts and I looked back on my life as if I was suddenly removed from it. The first thirty years of my life had been full of growing pains: my fathers death, a troubled childhood, a struggling single mother, frenemies, broken hearts, and having to endure the kind of Hell to be with my soulmate that made all of those prior painful experiences look small in comparison. Being handed the kind of life I had been given had never been easy, but I had made the best of it – and I was proud of myself. I knew that my father was too.

The cycle had been broken and I had done it all by myself. In that moment, I found full closure in my past and I knew I couldn't have gotten through any of it without having faith. I had survived all of those struggles and I was officially embarking on a new life for myself. It was the end of that story and the beginning of something much, much better.

Acknowledgments

Thank you Jen, for reading the first draft and having a sparkle in your eye when you gave it back. I knew then I had a story I could put out into the world.

Thank you Donette, for your encouragement. I hope you know how wonderful you are.

Thank you Marisa, for guiding me through this process. I looked up to you when we first met and I still do.

Thank you to those loyal friends of mine who have given that word meaning. I will forever praise every single one of you.

To my family, I'm thankful to share our bloodline, our thick hair, and our history. To my in-laws, I couldn't ask for better.

Thank you Mom, for **everything.** Home is where you are. You will inspire every hero in every story I write.

To the love of my life, my husband Jim, thank you for supporting me through this writing journey emotionally, spiritually, physically, financially and in every other way that there is. I couldn't have done this without you by my side. **You** are the happy ending. I love you to Cyberton… and back.

To my guardian angels/the brightest stars in my sky: **shine on.**